Unexpected Bargain

Episode 2
Of
The Missing Shield

Copyright

***

First Edition published in Great Britain, May 2018.
ISBN - 9781912648023

Publisher L. L. Thomsen
Edited by Lesley Neale, ReVise Editing Services

***

Visit the author's official website at

https://www.llthomsen.com

Or visit

https://www.facebook.com/themissingshield/

***

Contents

Copyright 3

Contents 5

Acknowledgements 7

Head's up From the Author.. 9

The Story So Far.. 11

A Captain, Enchanted 13

Dealings in Dust Town... 32

Solancei's Memoirs.. 48

She Says She Wills it! You Know You Want it!................. 49

Harkubsah's Place 58

Where You Will Find Only Ashes 72

Solancei's Memoirs.. 86

A Scent of Something Old – And of Something New 89

Unease in Friendly Territory 100

Solancei's Memoirs.. 111

Unexpected Bargain 114

Back on the Road... 123

Not Even a 'By Your Leave' 139

Solancei's Memoirs.. 149

Dreams of Jackals.. 151

A Gift of Foresight 164

Imprisoned... 177

Post Script from the author 191

Acknowledgements

This one goes out to all the fab critters who inhabit the world of social media.

Thank you to all my brilliant Twitter followers for brightening up my days and for sharing your life and experiences with so little hesitation. Thanks for the re-tweets and the hearts and the comments; thanks for the # games and the know-how and support. You are all much-valued and appreciated.

To all of my Facebook gang – most notably the 200 rogues! If I am ever stuck I know where to go! You guys and gals rock – watch out world: there will be some brilliant fantasy writers coming at you soon!

To my husband for his patience and everlasting support that helped me realise my goals and dreams. Though not a geek and fantasy lover like myself, your trust and generosity means the world and this work would simply not have been possible without you.

And finally, I can of course not neglect to mention the most important people of all: my children; my muses; without whom my imagination would undoubtedly still be slumbering in a deep subterranean cavern. When I spend hours at the computer you still cheer me on – never lose the magic!

Head's up From the Author:

Hi there and thank you for hopping onboard. Again.

I just wanted to let you know that I have deliberated (again) and decided that I would not clutter up this book with the usual array of maps, inventories or glossaries.

Now it's (still) not to say I don't love these things. As a matter of fact, I feel every self-respecting fantasy book should have something to support the narrative – because it's fantasy after all!

So with that in mind, I would (still) like to direct your attention to my official website www.llthomsen.com where you may explore titbits about the world of Dallancea at your own leisure, as well as look up names, terms, maps, information about the series and of course about yours truly, also.

The journey has only just begun, but I am immensely honoured that you have decided to come along. If you have liked it so far, there's lots of good stuff to come…

The Story So Far

➢ The Guardians have awakened to find their power reduced. The death of Second-in-Command Guardian, Envalair, is a heavy blow to the Upper Circle, but worse is the loss of their Sight, as is the broken magic and the sundered ancient Astrolabe, which is missing.

➢ First Guardian Malandar Cor'Esardan Denarlin has travelled to the Human realm of Ostravah in search of a link to the fated Twins – the Humans who are needed to help locate the shards of the missing Astrolabe, and who will be charged with wielding this artefact to re-calibrate the Veils of Time. Much lays altered across the realm, however, and so far he has only picked up the trail for the Tarvia – otherwise known as The Key. The presence of an illegal source of magic (a Neidar Ba'raie), may yet prove to be either the answer to his problems, or a magnet for their enhancement.

➢ Solancei, Duchess of Ivanor, cousin and Shield to Princess Iambre, has disappeared after fighting a duel in the backstreets of old Zanzier Town. At heads with the Princess over issues of behaviour and duties, her disappearance may yet prove of a personal nature, but it may also be linked to the foul developments that punctuated the jackal fight. So far Chief Eso, Solancei's mentor and Iambre's Head of Security stands without a lead either way.

➢ Worried for her friend, and for the revelations that this jackal fight was not the first attended by her Shield, Iambre now fears for her friend. If she has broken her oaths as a Shield, it will not look good for Solancei, but if made common-knowledge that her Shield and handmaiden has broken the laws to pursue illegal sports, this news could spell personal disaster for Iambre. With Solancei facing capital repercussions either way, for now Iambre must trust in the Chief's skills to straighten out the mess. A banquet awaits…

A Captain, Enchanted

She was without a doubt the most alluringly beautiful woman in all the realm! Or, at least, that was how Bilandro Metavo saw Iambre, Heiress to the Ostravahn throne, now that he finally lay eyes on her again after their time 'apart'. *Gods stand witness - and if the day itself had proven a dark and dreary disappointment, Iambre in the flesh was certainly anything but.*

It had a disturbing effect on his otherwise impeccable equilibrium. It had been that way for some time now and though the Gods only knew it wasn't getting any easier, Bilan still tried to swallow those wretched feelings.

He was semi-successful – something that only served to heighten his chagrin. *Iambre must surely to the Gods be aware!*

But how was he to succeed? It was no foul lie to say that he'd been anticipating this moment all day. In fact, since he'd been informed at first light that he would be her acting escort for the evening banquet, he'd been restless and impatient. Did it not now seem wrong that he wished himself far away?

I am mixed up, he thought, *and surely making a grand fool of myself! Play forgiveness and leave; that seems a good way of salvaging some dignity, but-*

Bilan swallowed painfully. He was here now; right where he wanted to be, of course. And in spite the danger of him breaking almost every protocol in the book, there was no point in regrets, for he was hardly going to leave the Realm's only princess stranded without an escort and he'd simply have to live with his own painful performance.

Live with it? Well indeed! Here he was: gawking when he should be making his obedience; wondering how to make things better between them, when he should not dare to think the thought - rats, but if the King could see, His Majesty would flay him for poor conduct! *Flay him and worse…*

Bilan grimaced. Well, at least he still owned a semblance of time-keeping. At least, he'd presented himself along with the four statutory guardsmen to form the appropriate escort as ordered – a little too well on time maybe, but just one stroke before the hour of quiet prayers, and therefore most assuredly not late…

Bilan would have smiled at his own eagerness: but in truth, it was pathetic, for in truth it was just as poor time-keeping to arrive early as it was to arrive late, but he couldn't very well just have stood outside as though he had no purpose, either. Indeed, he was the one who'd marched them all here like they'd been charged to relieve a century of battle-worn men about to lose a position of strategic value – and… *and he needn't have done that, of course; for fleck sake, he shouldn't have done that, but-*

Bilan flicked the thought aside. He supposed that he could've made them run, which of course would've seen him lose every shred of his hard-won respect with the men he commanded – so on that basis, he also supposed he still had a right to celebrate one small victory, but give it just a few more weeks…

No! No one would ever realise the state of him, and that was the key! And if he'd been early, Iambre's shy, young handmaiden had answered the door promptly regardless. *Good! It was all good!*

Bilan tried to focus on the fact that the sight of Palea had been a surprise. The slight woman already wore the customary light veil that one associated with a royal retainer, but though it successfully served to softly obscure her facial features, her short stature gave her away as surely as her face would've done. Iambre only travelled with three maids of honour and they'd been on the roads for a long time: Bilan recognized each easily by now – as did everyone else for that matter. Mistress Ina was a treat to the eye, of course, but Palea was his favourite – perhaps because of her quiet, almost-eviscerating 'servitude', which never seemed to falter - now where 'the Viper' Solancei had currently slithered off to was anyone's guess, yet always the one to get in the way, he fully expected her to appear at any moment.

'Iambre's Bane', he'd secretly dubbed the difficult woman for she was always there whenever he was anywhere near Iambre: watching him... interfering...

Bilan shook his head in wonder. *To find Solancei presently absent was a rather welcome relief; a relief that he tried not to linger on for too long because it opened possibilities...*

He quenched the unsettling thought and smoothed his face; the handmaiden Palea knew him by now and since he'd been expected, she'd allowed him entry without caution or remark, and where Solancei's greeting would've been tepid - *a mere inclination of her chin so as to offer him his title's due and not a straw's worth more* – Palea's had been 'court-conduct' personified. *Maybe...? Maybe the Viper was not around? Dare he hope, or...?*

Bilan stared at Iambre Actarione where she stood, halted in the door to her inner chambers by her handmaiden, so to oblige the woman with one last fiddly detail. The Viper was indeed markedly absent and he was suddenly happy his men could not see him. Sure, Palea might be pretty in a porcelain doll kind-of-way, but within a speck of time, he was aware only of the princess and the way her presence seemed to make his heart glow. *Alluringly beautiful... yes, she certainly was that without a doubt or contest - but it was more than that, which drew his eyes and heart. So much more...*

Sadly it was not a new realisation though it still happened to slash its way through his mind a grand total of exactly three times, whilst he watched the two woman bend their heads to rearrange the wide mesh of filigree gold that sat across Iambre's waist like a girdle.

What look might she afford him today, he wondered in one infinitesimal beat of the heart: the one of blazing disappointment? Or the light of betrayal that seemed to have been there whenever she'd look at him since-

Iambre lifted her gaze. Their eyes locked and suddenly the world was a blur because the tender expression on her face was unexpected.

Flushed hot and cold, Bilan's breath caught raw in his throat. Somehow he managed enough self-control to breathe out. *Somehow...*

Iambre held his gaze as though they were moulded together and for un-noted heartbeats, they both remained thus: immobilised; locked by each other's presence. Then she slowly pushed past Palea with a sideways murmur of thanks and his heartbeat seemed to explode like a thunderclap in his ears.

I should do something, he thought; *dumbstruck.* Decorum and protocol held him not five paces inside the gilded salon, but now that the Princess was in proximity, at the very least her presence demanded that he must bow - however, his body was presently unwilling to comply with statutory requirements. He waited for the change in her, but her face was carefully composed - and yet... the way she looked at him... *like she was part-scared, part-penitent, part-troubled, part-*

Suppressing a sliver of wholesome need, Bilan blinked. *By Jethar'Chi, if the King could see him now, indeed! Past relations and deeds aside, King Kaimar would flay the meat from his bones, then hang him, then do something obliterating to the rest of his remains – quite possibly without killing him first!*

He suppressed another shudder at the thought of his monarch's wholesome wrath, were the man to learn how his trusted Captain's lusted for his only daughter, but as if the world stood in mockery of propriety, Iambre chose that very moment to blush and smile.

A small familiar twitch at first, it grew slowly with some kind of secret knowing, chasing away what other emotions he'd just spied and suddenly he felt stupidly relieved. *Mercy… she was not angry. He'd felt sure she would still be, but that smile…*

Somehow he should not have been surprised, but he was. *Suddenly she was close enough to touch: suddenly-*

Protocol dictated that she should've waited graciously for him to regain enough of his wits to approach her to within the statutory three paces, but decorum appeared to have gone a-hunting unicorns in the woods because he remained foolishly mesmerised - and Iambre was definitely not shy about her personal space. *He should kneel; he should look away – holding her eye was too bold; he should-*

Iambre paused an arm's length away, the floating bronze fabric of her skirts rustling slightly and emitting a hint of Iddian meadow flowers and rose – the scent, he'd long since learnt to be her favourite. It was alarming to realise how much it felt like… *like home.*

Resisting the urge to reach for her as though he had the right, yet not trusting his own will, Bilan forced himself to think of 'home' then; real home that was - not the one he'd made for himself in Etruia as Captain of the King's Legion - but the former one: filled with shite, and filth, and crime, and it helped remind just where he'd come from and where exactly he did not have the breeding, nor authority, to go!

As ever, the sour perspective helped some, but not quite as well as usual. Iambre was almost tall enough to look him straight in the eye and nevertheless, she seemed only slight as she stood before him. *She was much too close for comfort; indeed much too close for the level of greeting he warranted...*

Bilan's hand had moved minutely of its own accord before he managed to wrench a better grip on himself. These feelings she inspired were dreams wrought of gold dust, cobwebs and air – alluring, useless and foolish! *What the fleck was he doing?*

He shifted an inch on the spot, uncomfortably self-aware. *He was riding too close to the flecking abyss - that was what he was doing! Too close for comfort, too close for sense, and yet-*

Wrenching a hold on himself, he tore his gaze from hers. *The King would have his guts! This was the flecking Heiress! It didn't matter whether she was angry or happy with him – it didn't matter...*

As though something released him, Bilan belatedly took a knee, respectfully bowing his head. That he knew he should have done this within a blink of seeing her, didn't help though, because he also knew that if he'd but retained just a sliver more of his former self, he mightn't have cared about rules, and honour, or anything else he'd once found so stupidly banal.

He'd changed though! Changed for something better! Yet now bloody Iambre Actarione was making his newfound adult persuasions waver, not least because whenever he was around her, he had the re-occurring inkling that she wouldn't much mind if he slipped.

With an inward curse, Bilan prized his thoughts away from that subject too. *There had to be something wrong with him. Or maybe the Gods had cursed him? The King had awarded him more than he could ever have hoped for: position, honour, trust... and this was how he repaid him? With illicit thoughts of taking Iambre on whatever plush bed, he knew to be behind that bedchamber door, and fuck her till he cried? With dreams of spiriting her away and keeping her for himself until the Province of Tuxama was no more?*

Bilan swallowed hard. *Traitor in thought but not in action! Wanting and doing were leagues apart and he must never move a muscle, because if he did...*

Sucking in each careful breath, he tried not to think, but even staring at the hem of her dress where it skimmed the floor, her face haunted his mind's eye; her body-

He blinked rapidly. *Holy Inkar'Chi! He had to stop this! Stop it now!*

Overcome by whipping regret to be thinking such thoughts to her face, a semblance of 'self' returned to him. *He was supposed to champion her - not mentally assault her. Gods, why could he not just get past this?!*

Suddenly beset with embarrassment at his own crude behaviour, Bilan finally managed to rouse control and apply it; a cough later, and his voice seemed to fall back under command too.

"Your Grace, Honour and Respect: as you command, I live to serve!" It wasn't lost to him how late he'd been in speaking the traditional words of greeting and fealty, nor was he unaware how his voice carried a gruff edge, but at least his eyes stayed irreversibly trained to the floor. *For mercy, protocol stipulated that he could not look up now until she gave him leave to do so - it was 'safe', and-*

An exasperated sigh met him from above, a ripple of tantalizing colours trailing across her skirts as she moved. It was all the warning he received, next she'd suddenly bent forward to place a warm hand beneath his chin.

Breath hitching, he just accurately managed to stop himself from jumping with surprise under the unexpected touch. *Kaimar will flay you! Kaimar will flay you! Kaim-*

"Captain, I thank you for attending,-" her clipped Etruian voice cut into his mantra, quiet but sweet: aristocratic, but with a hint of amusement, "-but you had better not be acting like this for too long."

"Protocol,-" he managed to croak. She sighed again, then gently forced his head up to look him in the eye.

"I hear your greeting Captain,-" *her eyes sparkled though the words were solemn,* "-and now it pleases me if you would stand."

Letting go of his jaw, she straightened once more as he moved to oblige her with wooden lack of grace.

"Palea," she addressed the handmaiden casually, eyes still on him, "please would you be good enough to tidy the dressing room. We have a little time before duty requires our attention and I have matters of importance to discuss with the Captain."

Things to discuss? For an impossibly long moment, he froze in astonishment, every muscle growing rigid. *Gods help him! She was dismissing the handmaiden. Gods...*

Bilan looked at Palea over Iambre's shoulder - *hoping she'd stay?* - and sensed the younger woman smile pleasantly behind the veil.

He quenched a curse. Somehow, when you spent so much time around people of royal birth, you soon got used to the nuances; the 'feelings' in the air. Palea was flecking going to oblige her lady; even if it was not exactly proper, she was going to oblige! Travelling had made everyone lax - campfires and tents did not lend themselves well to the long-term upkeep of finesse and stature; by now everyone knew each other and a certain disposal with propriety had ensued. *Gods and the Viper was still absent...*

As Bilan looked back at Iambre, just a shadow of weariness passed across her carefully made-up features. He might easily have missed it but…

The Captain straightened surreptitiously. Something beyond her and him troubled: he saw her gaze go vacant as she eyed the exit doors with a sudden hint of concern yet then shaking her attention back into place, and they watched in silence as the handmaiden left as requested.

For mercy, he supposed Palea managed to keep a sliver of decorum alive by failing to close the white-and-gilt doors behind her retreating form - *the Viper would not have left at all* – and if an open door was not much, an open door was still just what he needed. *It would keep him grounded. He hoped.*

Bronze-painted lips glistening, Iambre faced him, smiling in… *was that relief?* "There! Now that is much better, is it not Captain Metavo?"

Bilan hesitated.

"Captain," she nudged with gentle reproach, "Bilandro… please?"

Bilan glanced at the open doors and kept himself stiffly correct. *This was no time to get ideas, no matter the woman's tone! Even if Palea was clueless about many things, at least on the whole she had good instincts when it came to observing etiquette. If he could only take a leaf out of her book, everything would go smoothly tonight.*

"Crown Princess, you have official matters for us to discuss?" he observed, prompting her to recall her words to Palea.

"Hmm… yes…" Iambre's smile did not waver, but another shadow of something he would have named 'less assured' flickered into her amber gaze. Then she sighed. "Bilan… I… I... *we* need to talk."

Talk? Bilan felt a shiver race through him. *When last they'd 'spoken' it had been a disaster…*

"Your Grace, forgive me… about what?" Bilan kept his voice pristinely level but the question was there regardless as he added, "There is nothing to report. Your staff is safely and happily installed into quarters and bunks. It did not take long after-"

"Bilan stop." Iambre looked at him with unease but also a sting of determination. For a beat she seemed set to say one thing, then that odd shadow passed over her features again - *worrying him* - and when next it cleared, she simply said, "Come."

Displaying no reserve, the Princess grabbed his hand, offering no choice as she steered them both towards a small seating area by the heavy drapes now shutting away both the fall of evening and the rain-weighted clouds.

"Your Grace," he tried again but she only shook her head in denial.

Turning as she reached the two high-backed chairs and a small round table sheltered in privacy by three large pots containing a selection of popular green-leafed tall-grasses, Iambre indicated towards the left seat that he should oblige her and sit.

He did. Slowly and barely able to hide a frown. The woman could not be second-guessed, but part of him feared what she wanted; part of him craved it. The last time she'd looked at him with a smile, it had been when he'd gone to her, intent on apologising for his conduct at a prior event, but it had ended badly and instead of words of apology, he'd spoken some ill-received truths. From that unfortunate point, it had of course not been long before he'd been voicing some equally ill-received advice about how she ought to act, so that she might rectify their 'situation' - *his and Iambre's, not the retinue's* - with minimal damage, and well…

It had been a likewise ill-advised move on his behalf, he'd already known as much as he'd ultimately spoken the words that made her face fall.

He'd thought it all for the best - only she had not! And so she had punished him for 'his cruelty' from then: banishing him from her presence, using only third parties as go-betweens to convey orders, written or verbal. *That event had happened just over fifteen days ago now; too hard; too cursed long to see her only from afar and be allowed never a touch, never a look, never-*

"Bilan, I…"

Clasping her hands together, she stared at him with a hint of embarrassment from across the ridiculously small table separating them. Her perch on the edge of the other chair looked uncomfortable - her leaning slightly forward a precarious struggle as if gravity pulling her towards him didn't ride well; as though she was spooked and might dash at the wrong word or move.

"Bilan I am sorry!" she burst out, holding his gaze just a blink longer than needed so that he could not doubt her sincerity before she pulled away, issuing a small sound. As if she could not decide where to look suddenly, her eyes darted around the salon, eventually landing on an ugly tapestry depicting a scene from the Chaos Wars but Bilan barely noticed her discomfort.

She was sorry? How?

Milady?" he questioned - slightly numb with something he realised must be shock - and when she did not answer, he questioned louder, "Milady?! Please… what-"

"I am sorry for the Wilderness, and I am sorry for hurting you!" she bit out with ugly vehemence.

Wringing her hands like a vendor that had promised one price, now pushed to admit her goods might not be top quality, she appeared oddly torn as her eyes ripped back to his.

Venom gone in a flash, hardened battle commander emerging, she said, "I was foolishly craven and needlessly mean when I should have listened to sense, but... but you are always so damn chivalrous, and Solancei is always so bloody right!"

Bilan stared, taken aback by the language and condemnation, but he did not get a chance to speak.

"Gods know it is not much of an excuse," she carried on, sounding bitterly upset, "but between the two of you, it's... it's madness! Some days my head is about to implode with all your good intentions, and I am sorry. I just snapped. Even with my laughable attempt to delay us, even with our run of poor luck – which might I add, is verily not your fault at all – but yet-"

Iambre shivered violently, a half-mad expression pulling at her face. Then she exhaled and appeared to draw on her reserves. "I... that is to convey... we... well, we will soon enough reach Tuxama regardless of delays and harsh truths. It... I..."

With a worried glance for his silence, she begged, "Please, I am dearly sorry Bilan. Please... please say something."

Bilan shook his head, mildly confounded. *She was apologising? To him?* It was a selfless admission of fault, and one he appreciated, certainly, but she was the Heiress whereas he was just a star-blinded idiot who wanted to touch the sun, yet knew he could not do so and not die.

"Milady..." Bilan broke their eye-contact to look at his dark-tanned hands, strengthened since early youth to deftly delve into places they did not belong and in later years calloused by more than reins and sword-work. It made him feel ancient to think that whilst she got measured by three doting seamstresses and had been offered the choice between gold or silver hairpins, he would've stolen the very same from the Three Spirals beyond

Imkarah's infamous Lake Side district. *She did not know this, but he shared her apprehension in regards to Tuxama, for what would happen?*

He rubbed a finger over a cracked thumbnail. *He'd rarely been scared, let alone petrified. 'Petrified' was for the stories - except these days he was flecking petrified and then some!*

He rubbed harder as though the pressure might magically mend the split in both nail and spirit. In his own twisted mind, he currently coped with the idea of Tuxama because he *had* changed; because he *had not* moved on his desires, but-

But Gods, he knew she wanted him to. Without thought for future or consequence, she wanted him to! *And yet if… If he bedded her and played at calling her his for even a single day, he was not sure he would not kill to keep her…!*

Bilan closed his eyes, trying to order his thoughts.

"Bilan?" she insisted, sharply, with a sliver of dread now.

Hesitating just a blink longer, he exhaled painfully. Opening his eyes to hers, he said, "Milady, I thank you for the considerate words of apology, but truthfully, it makes no difference to the things that we disagreed on."

"Yes, it does," Iambre argued, leaning further forward, beseeching with both eyes and presence. "Bilan, I know what must happen. It is my duty, but Gods… how… how could you think me fickle enough to simply send you away – to send you back to father and Servangar as though it would make it all just a distant memory of… of me? Of… of us? Gods Bilan, I could not send you away: I love you!"

"Princess, no!" Aggrieved, Bilan shot to his feet. Locked between sweet conflict and terror, for a moment he towered above her like an expert mime tethering on his finale. *I love you…*

Iambre had never spoken so candidly before. The words did not seem to make sense and yet…

And yet he knew them true because the Gods had cursed him to feel the same way about her.

Illusion of stone shattering, he gulped-in a breath but felt suddenly sick. *This was not fair!*

"I know you want me." Smoothly regal, Iambre sifted to her feet, the soft light of candles springing flashes of wealth off her gown and jewellery; off her hair. As if she saw the truth in his face, she smiled: that beautiful, bedazzling smile that made him forget anything and anyone but her.

"Is it really so bad to admit that you want to stay with me? Tell me Captain: is it?"

"Milady, you don't understand. It's-" Bilan bit back the words, suddenly afraid of his own explanation and retreated clumsily, as she drew close enough to once more reach for him. *If she touched him…*

Iambre only smiled. She looked pleased then. *Not so much a Princess and more the-*

Somehow, just like that fateful day they'd first met, he was unexpectedly 'aware' of everything about her. Just as it had been then, the mask of make-up did not serve to erase the truth of her emotions and at this moment she looked as raw as he felt. *If he should pose the damning question would she go with him and never look back?*

A desolate feeling of longing swept through him. He feared the answer she might give but would never endeavour to ask. But if he did… where was the harm in asking just once…

'Just once'. It was the kind of conviction that would prove his downfall, wasn't it? *The knowledge, that he could snap at any moment and see propriety take flight! A kiss or two was one thing, but to go further-*

And then who could live like that? Hunted… hated… outcast…? The Princess of Ostravah belonged only one place! How could he condemn her to such a life? *Gods help him, but he couldn't. And he wouldn't.* Bilan swallowed but found his mouth gone dry. He was not as ignorant as most men when it came to women. *Gods, but he'd run away from women with that exact look of desperation about them when they'd clamoured to make him stay - and yet with Iambre…*

But there was never a cat's whisker of a chance that this would not end badly! It was only a question of degree, so no!

Navigating the chair's arm-rests, Bilan took another step back and noted her disenchanted frown. *Hurting her was hard, but protecting her was heartbreak. If she pushed, then-*

At the thought, Bilan almost backed up another step. He should simply speak to her now. Tell her more of the things she didn't want to hear: shatter the illusion. *Usually, the challenge lay the other way around; usually he'd tell them things they longed to hear, but not this time!*

Yes… what he ought to do was to drive the wedge firmly back into place between the two of them so as to make certain now, that she left his side this evening feeling only anger and aversion. *Yep, that's what he should do: make her hate him even more than the last time and once and for all kill that light in her eyes…*

Breath sawing on a deep inhale, Iambre seemed to steady her emotions. She looked at him and for a heartbeat, her face - so cleverly powdered, so charmingly enhanced - showed him only an odd caricature of the woman he loved. Oddly she wore more of the powder stuff than usual and he regretted the loss of her natural, clean beauty: the elegant brows, the almond-shaped eyes with the dark-tipped golden eyelashes, the pretty sloping nose, the full wide lips...

"Bilan, I missed you." Iambre offered, her tone just the right mixture of breathy honesty and desire that seemed to bewitch him – and there she was again: the woman beneath the title and the powders; the way she moved... *some people would've called it elegant, he'd call it something else entirely!*

"I missed you too," he heard himself say and saw the smile of his downfall return.

"And... you might forgive me?" she pushed, settling a palm on his chest.

Bilan startled and felt his head scramble up.

"There is nothing to forgive, Milady," he heard someone whisper past the rush of his blood.

Iambre sighed happily and stepped into him. Mildly reproving, she purred, "Captain Metavo, I thought we were past these official titles when in each other's company. Please... I have a name, or did you forget?"

Bilan shook his head, staring at the swag of heavy drapes as if something within might save him. The smell of her perfume in his nostrils seemed to numb his thoughts. *Rose... with a hint of something lighter; intoxicating...*

Part of him made a final, valiant effort to extricate himself from this danger - this was his moment, she was already half-expecting him to do this; this was the chance to tell her that she must send him away; that she must call for del'Draventar to act the escort in his place, and if...

Well, if he could push her away right now, he might make her mended goodwill shatter again, but the Gods had cursed him!

"I am so very sorry for our lost time, please forgive me?" she muttered against him as if he hadn't already said the words to reassure her, and she continued, "Bilan, I need your understanding. It's been hard. I was a fool and I have felt so alone; missed you so very much."

"Iambre, please, we cannot-" he tried, but she found his hand and squeezed it in hers, stalling his attempted distance, once again reminding him of the first time they met... *really met.*

Of course, most people living in or around Servangar could not have avoided seeing her from time to time - *she was the Princess* - but the Seat of Power was a huge place and until *that* tournament in Camporia, he'd never been 'fortunate' to set eye on her.

He'd known what they said about her though - but had paid it little mind. The realm was full of pretty, desirable lasses with soaring wits to match equally soaring fortunes and wily temperaments. *What had he cared whether he'd ever clap eye on the flecking Princess of the Realm or not?* To him it just hadn't been a matter of interest: his prime concern mainly evolving around the challenge of living up to the trust and responsibility so graciously bestowed by the King, and...

Well mercy, but the tourney field in Camporia and her subsequent invite had changed all that! Gods be good, hadn't it just! 'Moonstruck', they called it...

Bilan felt his own treasonous fingers weave themselves in with Iambre's to bring her hand to his lips for a soft kiss and she sighed against him. *Moonstruck...*

As he recalled Camporia only too well, he hadn't been the only 'offender' – like the famous beauty of her mother Queen Ishjah, Iambre lived up to expectations – and the entire time, other men would glance her way with varying degrees of adoration, hunger, and flirty cheek, and Bilan's own curiosity had been the least of it.

Had they all fallen in love with the Heiress that week?

Undoubtedly!

Had he set out to catch her eye?

So abso-bloody-lutely not - the mere audacity!

But it had been such random timing: him being there at the same time as the Princess; him winning the final tournament, snatching the honours right from underneath the much-celebrated Earl of Elarion's very fine nose; her - and not the local magistrate's daughter - presenting the trophy...

He had not realised till much later that she had been watching him too, courtesy of his name and what she'd known about the circumstances that had awarded him the Captaincy of the King's own Legion, but when she'd handed him that trophy...

Till this day he could not recall what the prize had looked like. A cloud of magic had enveloped him, or some kind of venomous spell had found the wrong target, or...

Inhaling her scent now, he stupidly wished he'd mirrored the Earl of Elarion. He should have saddled his horse on that hour to take instant leave of the place just like the young noble had done. He also should have neglected to call when summoned to her pavilion, but the fact remained that he hadn't left, and that he very much did attend!

A peculiar sensation sawed through him: perhaps a sense that none of this could've gone differently. It was stupid; he'd been stupid - and intrigued by her interest; flattered by her attention, and then...

A full hour in her presence - and he'd seemed unable to remember where his next breath would come from; two hours - and he'd been done for!

30

Good Gods… he should have saddled that horse! He should have saddled it and headed for the hills; he should have!

He should…

Dealings in Dust Town

First Guardian Denarlin lingered for a small while longer than intended, pondering Thessilia's reactions. Her objectivity seemed intact, yet he realised her feelings were still raw.

The loss of Marlan Envalair oozed from her soul, killing her in all but breath and heartbeat over and over, to the point where her remorse might shrivel her spirit and re-shape it into something foreign, into something less stable than an escaped Elemental...

The insight was disheartening, yet he held faith that she'd polish up focus to rekindle her former strength. Regret was for the dying or the deluded, reality ever the linchpin that kept most of his own sanity in check - and not even Marlan's demise could pull the blade on that - though as for the chaos of the fatal event, the betrayal, the sense of creeping, impending wrong...

Malandar resisted the need to look over his shoulder for an enemy he could not see. The Maker's runes were quiet. The strangeness surrounding his return to the realm had to be the culprit for his spidery-senses flaring without cause – *that, and the ruin that polluted the magic beyond understanding, of course.*

He pushed to his feet as if the fluid sharpness of the move might sever doubt.

A weak tingle at the back of his spine reminded of an enemy present yet ignored. He shook-off the resurfacing tendrils of wrath that had been brought to life earlier when his runes had abruptly awakened to alert him that the armed shepherds operating in pairs to guard livestock shadowed by wolfhounds, were present for reasons far more serious than some farmers' overly zealous need to defend against natural predators. *Venzoians!*

Impossibly, Venzoians hunted further south: not a solid presence to warn of an epidemic, but a presence of a couple – maybe a handful – which was enough.

Instincts narrowing, Malandar felt the subtle change come over him as the hunter within centred upon the link, the illegal 'presence' still gnawing at his bones like cold frost bite laced venom. But this was not the time. The people here seemed capable; he could not waste energy, nor power, nor cover, in favour of the poor return his dispatching of just a few renegade creatures might yield.

Relinquishing the fey allure of personal gratification, he exhaled the cauterising need and some of his tension lifted. He was still puzzled by the Venzoian survival though: the foul creatures were resilient, but they could not reproduce. He wanted to investigate, but feared his own persuasion if he got too close, so for the greater purpose, he refrained from scratching this itch too – again, since the Mad Ones would sense his presence in a heartbeat, and he did not have the magic to fight off enemies on multiple fronts. *Not yet. And still…*

An intrinsic hatred, born long before the Maker saw fit to grant Malandar rebirth, remained with half a withering tendril, *whispering, locked onto memories,* to dance on a spent breath and gossamer wings of shadow within him. *He should not leave the Venzoians. He really should not…*

Malandar tugged at the harness of the twin swords mounted across his back, resolutely punctuating wandering notions as he twisted the position of his satchel to ease his long-legged stride. By habit, he delved into thoughts of small things to waylay urges, yet the restless sensation lingered like a curse in the periphery just the same.

Leaving Venzoians to be culled by farm hands and dogs was not how he would have chosen to conduct himself; it was near border-line breech with the Maker's Laws; none of this was how he'd have chosen to carry on – and still...

His father's people were known to be gifted with prescience – Malandar had inherited none of this ability, yet he'd known too much not to see that worse was yet to come. The Circle hadn't touched on even half of it, but his fellow Guardians would have an inkling regardless, and if the Maker failed them now...

Unbalanced by the internal fight, Malandar knew a flare of discomfort. He was out of sync: felt bruised on the outside and weary within. Contradictions confounded, impatience snapped at his heels, considerations of foreign nature pushed at his peace of mind, twisting his equilibrium and offering no reprieve. He had ideas, but they were wrong – and not just because of their ill-design or chance of failure – but because of the catastrophe he might unleash, should his success by chance not be absolute.

For a blink, Malandar held a heartfelt wish that Marlan was still with the Circle to straighten this crooked sense of direction he seemed to be suffering. Yet as he pulled uneasily at the satchel again, he believed himself perhaps fortunate that his old friend *was not!*

In backlash, he experienced an instant, strange pang of honest regret that it had come to this; that it had come to these thoughts of disloyal honesty and hard candour. *Regrets that...*

A twisted smile tugged at his lips, something in him appreciating the strange paradox... *he was drumming up thoughts of regret, but he was not deluded nor dying - was he?*

Consigned to the company of ill-concerns, the First Guardian resigned himself to the present. He was making good headway towards the small town situated beyond the only rising hill; he could see the multiple streamers of what must be early-evening cook fires, all of them rising with fat, sedate purpose from what he judged to be a triple handful of chimneys just beyond the subtle ridge now. It formed puffs of undetermined clouds lower than the real thing: to proudly claim ownership of the underlying spicy scent of wood smoke in a way that most would associate with comfort and bliss after a hard day's work.

He hoped it meant he might be mounted before nightfall but the near-promise also brought the return of bustling impatience. So far the landscape had been forgiving: predominantly of flat terrain – easy to navigate even on foot - dominated by wide horizons, broken only by the occasional farm sheltered behind wheat fields and limestone borders speckled with age and red moss. *This was an area made for speed and catching-up time – he'd been left the opposite; if there were no horses here either…*

The dirt-packed road was widening slightly going up the slope, allowing for the progressive spread of a variety of hawthorns, malder and birch that gradually saw the former demarcation of landscape blur in favour of untended acres of virgin grasslands flecked like a painters smock with the occasional scattering of purple and red autumn blooms. It was not something he'd expected to see coming up on a town that purportedly prided themselves on housing no less than two equine vendors. *The season was late and most grazing surely cropped low by now…*

Feeling less than optimistic, Malandar walked on - his attempts at soothing the ruffled resentment still-harboured, now easily choked beneath considerations of a far more mundane nature than the questions of warping magic and shot senses.

This was already a tedious enough exercise in patience without adding the possible nuisance of misdirection to the fray and he hoped this was indeed the place local travellers had referred to when musing upon the subject of where to pin down the location of a horse-coper. Twice before he'd known disappointment, a small fact he'd deliberately neglected to pass on to Thessilia - and if he'd previously hoped people had been jesting a lone traveller into black doubt when announcements had forecast trouble purchasing any kind of horse in these parts of the fifteen provinces, Malandar had since then culled his optimism. Evidently, twisted local humour had little to account for and reality everything: no one owned a horse in these parts it seemed; of those who'd thought they might know of a trader, few had been certain of the exact town, but eventually he'd patched together this location. *Sadly, even with the aid of hearsay and history, it was undoubtedly his best lead for miles, and besides… what choice did he have?*

Malandar snorted softly to himself, wondering when he'd last been pushed to base sound strategy on hearsay? Horses would be better than going on foot though - and regardless of what the creatures lacked in pace in comparison with an Eikyr, they would conveniently serve to bolster his appearances too – something he hadn't previously thought to consider until other travellers had been drawn to his 'misfortune' like carrion to Draken'Dah left-overs.

As it turned out, the presence of his twin-swords notwithstanding, most imagined he'd been robbed, often leading them to pose an array of fearful questions about highwaymen or other questionable personages likely to be located en-route. *Pests were, his answers might have served to alleviate fears but they'd also made him memorable – something he most assuredly did not wish to be.*

Malandar exhaled and lengthened his stride again. He'd altered his looks, but the glamour did not hold well without the meticulous weave of specific flows and because of his persistent reluctance to expend the valuable power of his runes on 'trifles', there were glitches in the construct he'd

Persuaded. This, in turn, had made it a necessity that he'd regulate only his physical appearance, not his attire, for the underdone spell would flex with independent life and a flair for chance – all in all not great when attempting to avoid 'memorable'.

So apparently he'd been left looking slightly the eccentric Etruian noble – or an Esardan wander. The latter inspired vague amusement but not enough to excite forgiveness for the circumstances. Opinions couldn't be helped and the Maker only knew that existence had never been simple, so this was by no means a heartache, really - but this creeping around: this need for stealth?

By now he'd had to assure several people that he'd simply lost his mount due to vexing circumstances - *which was the truth after all* – however, even if it had served to relieve tensed-up faces and worried frowns, he was growing tired of the drill.

How had the weather conformed this summer in the capital? He looked pale – so his mountain-retreat must have provided adequate relief from the scorching sun? Did the Capital seem much altered with the absence of the Heiress? What was his destination? Did he recall the wine-merchant on Park Hill Boulevard? A cousin of a friend would dearly wish to know if the flavour of peach brandy was still in favour, or if the new apple-punch had taken precedent as predicted? And so on. And so on…

How long before his luck ran out? How long before somebody's random mention of a lone strange traveller somehow got picked up by the Agents of Chaos? He needed magic - more than the seed of Power residing in his runes could provide, but with the current flows…?!

His mind spun from thoughts of the one possible stop-gap solution that he'd shied from acknowledging ever since he'd found himself expelled from the Boundary, head pounding and bones hurting: on his knees in a small stream too shallow to sate a goat yet invasive enough to somehow still soak the ends of his hair and the best parts of his attire before wherewithal returned him enough mind to clamber onto dry ground.

He'd sensed the *Neidar Ba'raie* before he'd known of the Mad One's creatures; as with the Venzoians, instincts and Law demanded that he took appropriate action in regard to *this* discovery, only...

Only the action he was currently contemplating in regards to the Neidar Ba'raie seemed so far removed from the usual process that he felt sick just contemplating the extent of his luck.

So don't think yet, his mind jested with blank objectivity, *give yourself more time, cipher out more details about the current state of Ostravah and use it to look for alternatives.*

The First Guardian frowned. And just who was he fooling? One spicy truth he'd willingly related to Thessilia, had been the disturbing fact, that the people here no longer seemed to carry any link - and thereby memory – of the old past. It made them practically ignorant: a herd of grazing cattle too absorbed to notice the stench of danger that commonly preceded a pride of Venzoian Ranzar about to pounce. *Why assume that anyone would possess even a grain of wisdom to be moulded to his advantage? They could not help him and he could not help them. Not like this. Not yet. But if he was willing to run a risk, then maybe...*

Had the Upper Circle not always taken what it needed to satisfy the greater good, the future? And if there was no precedent now, was there at least not need for him to consider this... this deviation?

Unable to determine the truth just yet, the sketchy idea of what he might do left him faintly haunted but the new reality was shifting towards them under the influence of Chaos and couldn't be ignored either. No matter how he chose to deploy strategy, there'd be things he and the others could not prevent. The changes were too many and deep. A new clash between the Upper Circle and the Mad Ones was inevitable and this Human ignorance could easily prove an unpredictable reliability: something to cause hitherto unforeseen trouble not to mention far-reaching repercussions.

Of course, the Neidar Ba'raie could be the answer. Could. But his fellow Guardians would think him mad!

Yet, whatever he did, people were going to die regardless: their subsequent awakening to the truth would be terrible and might even throw the lands into internal strife and civil unrest. He did not know who would lead them back into the light after all this time, did not perceive of a way in which these lands might accept the idea of magic once the Maker had addressed and balanced the current issues. *The complexity… the old versus the new…*

The stench of incense and madness clinging to a near-by road-shrine broke Malandar of his dark thoughts as he crested the knoll in the road and spied the culprit: a simple altar of stone and wood erected under the wide poisonous crown of a tall heinar, allowed to grow from stunted shrub to full tree. *The air surrounding the setting seemed to shiver with invisible energy – cloying… dense… pulsing…*

As though he'd hit a barrier, Malandar halted, all further advance curtailed. Three simply-dressed townspeople knelt in the dust and shredded black leaves, praying before the make-shift alter laden with trinkets and food, some of which could be seen and smelt to have been left out in the open for some time.

Nose crinkling, he tried not to inhale, but feelings stirred. A little to the left a stacked pyramid of oranges could be spied sagging on itself like a collapsed dolls house, the decomposing odours drawing vermin and bad memories with their split, sickening yellow-green peel and sweetly noxious decay. *Over a quarter of a season, they must have sat there, people adding more…*

Strangely unbalanced by the sight, he swallowed back sudden sentient wrath: a sensation with a flavour of complexity he might easily abandon sense to pursue. He couldn't however. Words older than those sworn to the Maker slipped forth in a reminder of simple promises made - and it razed the uneasily-veiled sense of offence he might otherwise have unsuccessfully attempted to flatten under a broader blanket of simple 'prudence'. *Move. It was time to move…*

Slightly dazed, yet regaining his mind, he slowly unlocked his limbs, shifting and relinquishing the shape of an annihilating Persuasion of a spell left blistering in his mind like a split lip after a fist fight. *It would empty his reserves all over. No good. No need. People, just people,* his conscience appealed, sporadic like the dry leaves dropping from the heinar, *they were just people…*

Malandar clasped a hand around the front strap of the sword harness, a hiss escaping him as he forced feet to move and legs to take him towards the vulgar sight. *He'd passed shrines like this. It shouldn't matter. It shouldn't…*

As though they felt his presence, or maybe because they'd heard his vexed exhale, the three worshippers had sat back on their heels to look towards him as he drew nearer. His approach made them weary, he saw, the echo of their discomfort as evident on their faces and stiff limbs, as the nauseating field of disturbance to his spirit - and Malandar rapidly flexed the air he'd shifted to ensure the screen of illusion still held sway. *For mercy, the small trick hadn't failed though, for mercy…*

Concern allayed, he stayed himself from circling wide to pass the three people as though they were in fact the carriers of a foreign contagion. *Rarely had he felt so wrong. These people... they looked...*

Senses brimming, feeling the false God too near, Malandar forced one boot in front of the other.

The two women and one man did not appear impoverished, nor deprived. Like most people living on the edge of farming-communities-turned-towns, they wore common homespun: pale skirts and breeches, stout shoes, coloured shirts with frilly sleeves and stripes of red and green - the man alone the somewhat less-bold looking, in simple greens and a floppy wide-brimmed hat that shaded both short pale hair and much of his days-old beard. *There was nothing unusual about them; they looked... normal... yes... but... but their worship...!*

The First Guardian found it hard not to read treason in their presence, for their devout worship had invoked enough of their chosen 'God's' Spirit for Malandar to feel his personal affront bristle in the air as though made sentient. Meanwhile, the deity-of-choice in turn seemed to have evoked in the worshippers a sense of anxiety, courtesy of Malandar's unexpected proximity to the shrine. *This could escalate. If the God was touching them the mad creature might recognise his presence, but he mustn't let it...*

Yet, just as he could sense the presence drawn through the strength of their piety, so did they sense in him both a lack and strength of power that might reveal his true identity, and though the essence of the chosen deity could not touch him per se, it did not mean that it wouldn't try, particularly if it sensed something 'wrong'.

It made his imaginary hackles rise in preparation. *It would cost these people their lives and the Upper Circle the element of surprise. 'Escalate' was perhaps not the word...*

Malandar swiped his mind free of thought, closing and folding his spirit in on itself till he felt imprisoned in his own body but was also not radiating a footprint of magic. It partly worked but he could taste the confusion surrounding the shrine: as though the part-cognisant presence sought to recall something forgotten. It made it likely these people had invoked the essence of Osari'Chi the Veiled: a deity who often fell victim to his own faults, but unless the would-be God manifested and took them for Vessels, Malandar would of course not know for certain.

He hoped the Mad One would not gain a Vessel, but just the same the First Guardian did not yet trust in his own sustained anonymity. The youngest woman was staring with vivid amber eyes upon the hilts of his swords, her narrow face displaying an array of emotions that didn't seem to settle for long enough for him to read. Then a flex in the air made Malandar clench his teeth as Osari'Chi's essence seemed to slide through her, almost sealing her death-sentence - yet the insubstantial attempt fell short of success – releasing the woman as though power was lacking after all.

Instead, a fly buzzed from a dirt-besmirched bowl atop the slap-alter to settle upon the man's right cheek but he appeared not to notice. *The wrongness felt palatable and yet Osari'Chi didn't manage to make a claim. There was not enough Power, or maybe He lacked conviction.*

Hand quivering, Malandar forced it from the harness to rake back the wrought semblance of shorn golden-brown hair in need of a trim.

"Fair afternoon upon you and your town," he pushed out; perhaps too casually.

Operating a disarming smile that might only have worked because his illusion allowed it, he said, "Please, don't let me detain you from... from devotions, but...

"Well, as it were, I have been directed to your town by fellow travellers. My mount was indisposed, you see, and so I am looking to purchase a horse here. Might I perchance be in luck?"

The woman with the amber eyes blinked once, her face warming to life just as the other two shook themselves and the air seemed to lose its heavy scent; a soft, welcome breeze travelled down the hill, dispersing with the surplus of emotion.

"It is no trouble," the man said, looking puzzled to deny the truth of his words. Yet, swiping at the brim of his hat as though to see Malandar in a clearer light, he seemed sincere as he added, "We will need to complete our prayers, otherwise I would have shown you friend, but head on out through town and keep on the road for the next quarter of a mile. The big barn is easily spotted and if the old oaf has any nags to sell that's where you'll find them."

Malandar nodded. "And the other vendor?"

The man paused, looking blank-faced, but the woman with the amber eyes brightened. "Ah Gods, the other..."

No longer put out, she looked instead perplexed. "Well, Sieward never took time to pray, never took moments to offer respect, and so... well, I guess he was briefly touched by Osari'Chi, then he died. As for his stock...? Well, I cannot be sure but think it all went to Zanzier."

"My thanks then for your time." Malandar was already sideling past the people, cultivating gratitude and distance, but with a parting nod from the man they seemed to lose interest anyway and he marched off as they sunk to their knees amidst rot and old heinar leaves once more.

Ahead, gathered in a natural depression in the landscape, sat a middle-sized village, the dry main thoroughfare he'd been following, streaming straight through the line of two- and three-storied, white-washed, black-thatched buildings. It was not picturesque but it was not poverty stricken either: the roof lines looked perky, the trellis woodwork fresh: decorative rather than structural, and still...

After his near-encounter with Osari'Chi there was a stale sense of illness descended over the landscape, like an omen of dread, laced into the village: somehow rendered more obvious by the bleak slant of late-afternoon light that managed to void most colours, leaving everything a paler-than-usual parody of better times.

To Malandar it gave the impression that the road was nothing more than a canal of dust, slowly eviscerating and choking the life from the world, but other dwellings had been built to the back of the main run, their design solid.

It raised hope. And regret. Smaller, but still affluent-looking, some constructs had warehouses attached, others what appeared to be shops, but if it should have been an omen of prosperity, Malandar knew the town's misplaced piety would eventually suck all life from the place.

He spied a faded sign, barely visible behind a row of stunted bushes twenty paces out. As though a taunt to both past and future the flaked-off gold paint read: 'Dust Town, trading post, proud place of Chicken Farmers. Four-hundred-and-seventy-eight Gods Honouring Mortals'.

Though he tried, Malandar couldn't withhold a soft snort of derision. *Gods? Gods...?! The poor fools - not for all the magic in the world had the Maker's first children ever been 'Gods'!*

He wrenched his attention away from the sign, staring stonily at the road in front of him. As he went through the town, keeping to a line of relatively well-maintained boards that flanked the settlement to save the townspeople dusty hems on good days and muddy shoes on the bad, he met relatively few people.

It was near dinner time, he imagined, the assortment of smells sneaking out from upper floors and a couple of inns, enough to spare him the casual encounter that strangers invariably seemed cursed to endure in these kinds of places. However, traces of worship did not spare him the same courtesy; they were everywhere: in the name of a seamstress' lodgings, in the signs carved into posts or lintels, in the air.

He suppressed another hiss of consternation. *Some Humans had always suffered from gullible streaks, but this?*

Chewing on bad feelings and a smouldering, twisting demand that seemed to flex beneath his skin where the Maker had inked him with His runes of Power and Honour, Malandar resisted the urge to gag. *Old iron encircling his neck would've stung less than this! Was there not a reason these foul beings were known as the Mad Ones?! Silicia'Cha, Kira'Cha, Inkar'Chi, Jethar'Chi, Arbar'Chi - the name made little difference, but their sway had grown; people were going to die - in countless numbers - and the Mad Ones would be laughing in delight as the fools fell to their knees in prayer of succour and mercy!*

Flicking a skein of straight hair back over the shoulder with an impatient move, a long look received in exchange of a quick question put to a passing local, assured him that the stables were indeed situated on the far side of town and he stepped off the last board without interest for the way the extended panels of his ancient long-sleeved coat dredged up yet more dust.

In a slight hollow to the west, flanking the sloping edge of a good few acres of rising woodland to the south and open fields north, nestled the horse-coper's place as promised, the only parts currently visible, the line of an old gambrel roof. A quarter of a mile seemed a comfortable estimate, though at first glance it was a top line that had seen better days: a view that he did not deem worthy of revision as he eventually drew closer to the place.

Malandar paused in an open yard, scarred by cracked flagstones and brown tufty grasses, surveying the barn and surroundings with a sceptical frown as he shook the worst layers of dust from the sleek panels and sinuous lines of his once-costly coat, now temporarily turned from black to grey in equal measure to rival the recent dirt likewise deposited on his boots. As impressions went, he was alarmingly underwhelmed.

The place looked past its best; but for the scent in the air and the subtle sounds of horses from within the structure itself, the place might well have been shut to trade. *Were he to find a mount here, it might well be half dead!* He recalled the man at the shrine. *He'd referred to the owner as 'the old oaf'...*

Malandar thought he'd need nothing short of a spell to incite reason and insight into the man's blind worship of a creature that merited no honour, but he needed scarce imagination to comprehend the man's scorn of this establishment!

Utterly careworn, rickety fencing made up the perimeter of an empty circular corral to his left. The hard-stamped dirt within looked an infertile mauve - the few die-hard weeds surrounding it without, struggling to flourish against pealing posts. In many places the soil fractured by drought mimicked-well the crackled glaze of old china and with no horses to be seen in the surrounding fields of long waving grasses and blue thistles, he had to wonder what manner of trader this place belonged to; indeed he had to wonder if he'd be leaving here on two feet like he had the others?

He quelled a sigh.

A saving mercy perhaps, a sign hammered across two stumps of wood jutting from the barren ground did indeed proclaim the stables open for equine vending by courtesy of Master J. Harkubsah, but of course, the sign and the positively-faded advertisement might yet belie prevailing current relevance.

Still... *grasping at straws perhaps...* but for spite, 'Harkubsah' was a name of Deb'Aran origin – and as memory served, the Deb'Aranis used to breed good horses.

Yet these days... who knew?

Solancei's Memoirs

The Province of Tarléon.
Ocean's End.
Autumn of 780 P. C. W.

So with the funerary rites now completed, I was ushered with surprisingly small ceremony into the first white-lacquered, horse-drawn sledge that awaited by the edge of the grave site – the gaggle of fur-wrapped, chalky-eyed people I barely knew, all seemingly keen to get moving now.

Quite as if they couldn't soon-enough be away from the desolate place of the resting dead, the Funeral Prefect and some unknown advisers also scrambled immediately to accompany me. *It was by order of my father's steward Rainan, that they did so - but they looked happy enough to comply.*

I didn't blame them, though. Gods no, I didn't. The ever-present ice cap was an unpleasant reminder of one's own mortality in this harsh frontier province, which always took more than it gave. That day of all days, it seemed no one wanted to tempt the Gods; the driver cracked his whip, the horses responded without pause, stamping their metal-shod spiked hooves into the ice to find purchase - and then we were away.

As we sped across the silky-looking ice, I would have preferred Rainan's company of course, but as he was father's caretaker, he was charged to leave last - after the caskets had been covered and the shafts re-filled – and I only hoped they'd shift that small hill of ice quickly.

Even a child could see the weather would not keep, and I did not want to lose Rainan too!

Solancei

She Says She Wills it! You Know You Want it!

Bilan shook himself off the memories and wondered how the fleck he'd ended up here. As though the Gods had decided to mock him, the King had entrusted him with Iambre's safety on this journey, and curses! *Who better for that task than the man who'd demonstrated such loyalty to the throne? Yes... who, indeed? He would guard her with his life - and more!*

"So how have you been?" she enquired, her breath warm against his chest as she broke their quiet moment. "Did you miss me too?"

And what the fleck could he say...

The truth of it was that he should not have felt a thing. Gods, he had no right to miss her – none at all – and still...

Her anger had grated on him until he'd felt thinner than sheet iron. *How had he been? Mad from only seeing her from afar; from missing their conversations; from not touching her!*

"I missed you." Bilan's hand moved of its own volition to stroke her hair, then stopped, aware that he would ruin the careful coiffure, though casual it might look. It didn't seem to matter. At his soft admission, Iambre drew back from him a little and caught his eyes with a contrite frown for what seemed to be some kind of embarrassment.

"Bilan, my behaviour was unacceptable." She swallowed and her gaze flickered as she appeared to fumble for the right words. "And I... I am sorry to have provoked all the... well, for everything which happened. My judgement was not sound, nor my heart, but..."

"But, Bilan I swear... what you said to me...about us? Well, it was so maddeningly logical that it made me doubly aware that we... that this will soon end, and then..."

Iambre swallowed further words and looked away.

"Milady, it does not matter," he began but she looked up at him then with a startling expression of stilted wrath.

"Sweet Belanzia'Cha! Bilan it will never cease to matter! You scared me! I thought us already at odds about your *willingness* to act on your feelings and then you go and throw ashes at me! I lashed out! How does that not matter?! How does it not matter that duty and life will force us apart? How?!"

Bilan sucked in a careful breath and tried not to think of how much it very much *did* matter. *But it couldn't.* The jewellery on her neck and wrists was worth a small fortune, reminding him of just who and what she was. *The cut and style of her dress; her expensive scent; her flawless skin...*

There was a time he would have seen nothing but the monetary value of such riches but now he barely offered it a second look. He had long since come to understand without a doubt that she was not a woman of excess: as per usual, her beauty was complimented rather than outdone – and yet she was still the sum a hundred wondrous dreams. *She was going to the Banquet, not he. She was the Princess, he a random soldier, and still...*

Weren't soldiers known to do despicable things from time to time?

"Bilan!" she snatched at his attention with a searching look of concern. "We might not have long. You are scaring me again!"

"Not half as much as I am scaring myself," he told her with a salty edge and a sudden hot flare of need. *She was right: they did not have long. Not long at all...*

With an effort, he pushed himself away from her and she looked lost when he added yet another pace of separation.

"Bilan?" Iambre enquired as if pained. Haranguing her bottom lip with her front teeth, she seemed both unsure and at a loss as she considered him.

Bilan only drank the moment, willing himself to memorise details for later recall, but it sent his many feelings warring. There was the temptation to remove the two amber-encrusted pins holding up parts of her loosely curled tresses, so very unlike the usual Etruian-style of elaborate braids and complimenting ribbons - *or was that the Iddian style, now?* – he wasn't sure, but well... *rats whatever!* Other than the Kretorian, few women wore their hair loose, but tonight Iambre's hair brushed past her waist, the thick fall of it far longer than any Kretorian woman he'd ever known. *Yes, there was a terrible temptation...*

Resolve wavering, Bilan clenched his fists.

Hair like that, you could touch without messing up those artfully woven coils and miniature ornaments or fine silver chains she was normally wont to wear as symbols of status and fashion. Hair like that...

Bilan wanted to curse out loud to break this spell or whatever it was. *He hadn't expected to see her like this!* He could so very easily remove those pins, yes – but if he did, he would also have to run his hands through those white-golden strands before he kissed her, and-

Gods be good! Cut your own heart out then!

"Iambre, I cannot love you," he grated with a touch of frustration and more than a pinch of anger that he should even find it so difficult to do the right thing. "Princess, you must dismiss me now and call for Lieutenant Commander del'Draventar to act in my stead tonight, and tomorrow I will have to insist that you grant me leave to return to Etruia."

Iambre looked confused. Not the conceited kind of confused. *The painful kind.*

"Bilan?" Her voice was small. "Bilan please... please do not do this. You are here and I am here. We both know it feels right."

"Your Grace, just because something feels right, doesn't make it right. I don't want to go, but I think I should leave. For both our sakes."

Iambre looked undone. "No..."

Bilan pushed a hand through his hair to release frustration. "Please Milady, leaving you will be harder than it ever would've been to leave your father to pass on beneath the dirty blades of enemy daggers! If you know me at all, then you will know this is the Gods' own truth. And I swear it to you: it will kill my spirit to go, but-"

Bilan broke off sharply as his voice seemed to deepen with a hint of the madness boring into him. He must be lingering on the edge of insanity. He did not want to love this woman; he did not even want to be attracted to her, but he did and he was; irrevocably. He wanted to stay but no good could ever come of it. *He'd always known this; she knew this! Difference was that now he was as committed as a descending sword: unable to pull free from the trajectory he'd set upon. It would be best if she dismissed him again – and yet if she did...*

Her eyes were deep pools of liquid amber pouring into his and for a moment she looked so full of sorrow that he had to wonder if something else was amiss, yet then a change seemed to roll over her like a sudden mist from the hills to hide the fallen of a recent battle - and rejecting the notion, his spirit curdled. *Fleck... so this was it...*

Iambre drew herself up, becoming regal and untouchable, her personality evaporating behind the illusion of aloof disinterest and royal arrogance.

"Very well then." She paused to compose her voice, the illusion wavering before she managed to control it. "Bilan, I love you but if you truly wish for me to terminate your charge, then I will make it so. 1st Lieutenant del'Draventar is a very capable man, as is 2nd Lieutenant Mortrat. This Tour is nearly over anyway and I guess I was but foolishly hoping…"

Iambre's voice cracked suspiciously, but her eyes were void of tears. *Sanguine serenity, they could write songs to her skills, epics…*

Bilan drew a deep breath, making as if to kneel but she hissed in warning. "Oh don't you dare, Metavo! Don't you dare!"

Looking suddenly angry beyond thunder, Iambre flashed around the chair to stand before him. "I will discharge you Captain, but not yet. Not tonight, and-"

Iambre never finished her own words. She was too close; he could feel the heat riding off her presence - and then her lips were on his, sealing his surprise just as she caught a hold of him to stay flush against his body as he stumbled slightly beneath her onslaught. It stunned him for a heartbeat: he'd kissed her before, but…

It was like someone firing a heady drug directly down every inch of his body, awakening everything he'd hoped to bury, eroding every last rational thought under a feeling of utter disregard for anything but this connection. For a blink, he tried to pull back: for a blink-

Iambre broke the contact, her breath heavy, her eyes clouded, and her lips…

"Forgive me Bilan, I am a little out of sorts," she began, but Bilan couldn't seem to hear her properly. There was a storm brewing within him; his blood seemed on fire; his mind without reason…

'What Iambre wants, Iambre gets!' the handmaiden Solancei had once told him with disconcerting honesty whilst holding his eye with that alluring grey gaze of hers. *'You, Captain, should know this – and consider yourself warned! Stay the fleck away if you value your skin!'*

He smiled, semi-drunk on memory as well as the present.

Yes, the 'Viper' had a way of swearing that made her seem both threatening, regally aloof, and disapprovingly dismissive all at the same time - but he'd known she meant business; she'd been wearing no veil and her hostility had reeked from her, like frost from the ground in the depths of Kheltian winter. *She'd always been another suitable reminder; another deterrent; but now she was not here…*

Bilan was barely aware that he reached for the princess. The bold fire in her egged him on and yet he had the brief satisfaction of seeing her made-up eyes widen slightly with pleasurable shock as he clasped her waist and wrenched her close. Then she glided into his embrace, a perfect fit; within a blink, she'd clutched subtle fingers around his biceps, and…

'Stay the fleck away…' Solancei's words echoed. *Too late!*

Bilan kissed Iambre. It was like he'd never touched her before and yet they knew each other intimately. She kissed him back… *desire grew… flaring…*

And Bilan fell then, lost in her warmth as he returned her kiss. They were alone. Abstinence and long-held restraints seemed to overwhelm all good sense. Iambre pushed against him, moulding herself to his form as though she'd been made solely for his embrace and he conceded ground, barely aware as their passion led them in a tumbling dance past the plush chair he'd previously occupied.

Unsurprisingly, neither of them moved to break the kiss through; hands all over her, Bilan felt both blissfully gratified and savagely starving for more. *By the lustful Jethar'Chi, this was so wrong but yet so right! So, so right!*

Moving her hands over his back, up his neck and into his hair, Iambre seemed to cling to him and he shuddered with pleasure at her touch, even as she playfully bit his lower lip hard enough to stun.

Pain flared briefly, sweetly, but in the heat of kissing, of touching, he found it exhilarating; circumventing the low gilt-framed table without tripping over any of the protruding scroll-work, their passionate dance was brought up short only when they made contact with the heavy tapestry pecked to the wall.

The impact jolted. The frame rattled. Iambre exclaimed wordlessly in meagre protest but neither seemed bothered enough to separate. The rich thread on the wall-hanging might be several hundred years old and was certainly only meant to be handled with delicate attention - but care was swept from Bilan's mind before he could even understand it. *Let the moth-eaten thing split and fall to the floor!* He couldn't find concern. *Iambre was in his arms…*

Intensifying his grip, he spun them smoothly around in a tight circle to pin her back against the rumbled wall panel. Iambre knocked her head lightly in the process but moaned encouragement against his lips regardless, and he failed to stop. *Gods… and that perfume!*

Using the wall in support Bilan shifted his hold on her, smoothly encircling her bottom with one arm to lift her up off the floor and pin her closely to him, and she shifted easily to accommodate the change, boldly encircling his hips with silk-clad legs as her shimmering skirts rode high. *Mercy…*

Breathing heavily, she broke away from his lips long enough to trail kisses down his neck whilst his hand moved to push the rich fabric of her skirts further up. Somewhere within, somewhere far away, his inner voice roared for him to come to his senses but right then he could not have stopped himself from sliding his hands up her soft stockings, had an army been bearing down to assault. *She loved him!* He felt on fire; strangely drunk. *Sweet mercy, I should stop…*

Assuring him that the saint shouting on his shoulder was of no consequence, Iambre helped by approving his touch with a soft murmur against his neck before adjusting to find new kisses.

Her tongue in his mouth shot bursts of lightning through his loins. Jethar'Chi the Sinful egged him on. *He could just take her here and now – that was what they both wanted; they'd come close before - but had never done it - and the mere idea of it intoxicated!* She was malleable: a soft warmth in his embrace and she was clinging to him with a possessive yet vulnerable force, he'd never believed possible. All at once, she was hot and fiery and he could only dream how perfect her naked skin would feel next to his; all he had to do was take her; it would be easy, and-

And, it would be the worst thing he could ever possibly do – most of all, to Iambre herself! Mercy be hanged!

Provoking a semblance of rationality where none had existed, the thought scratched open something he'd locked away and as it belatedly crawled towards the surface, he became mindful of the hand on her left thigh; became aware of the way his own tense body crushed hers in readiness to complete their passion there and then.

The awareness parted the daze further. His right hand was readily posed to remove any hindering clothing in less than a few shuddering heartbeats: the insanity of their behaviour was sobering! *Gods…!*

The madness of his conduct and what it would inevitably lead to, should he so cheaply consummate his feelings, was like a splash of icy ocean water over his fire: all of a sudden, it was all he could do, not to drop her and flee the room. *She was the Crown Heiress!*

Clearly feeling the diminished passion between them, Iambre slowly pulled back to look at him.

It made him wince: her eyes still clouded from the heat of their embrace. *If only he could ignore it all! Hah! If only he had never met her!*

Reading his face, as she was so excellently versed in doing, she suddenly looked confused. An air of distress crossed her features as her own high dwindled, then died - *she understood but appeared not to accept… good Gods…*

Brow furrowing, for a blink she looked set to argue, but Bilan stalled her. *Just say the words… say…*

"No," he heard himself say, "No, this is not right! I am sorry, Milady… this is not right. This is my fault, I-"

Bilan cut his own words short. It all seemed like a bad dream.

Setting her gently back onto her feet was harder than holding onto hot coal with his bare hands but as her slippers hit the carpet beneath them, her skirts rustled to the floor and readily settled to hide her legs as if in mute agreement with his decision - and if he felt ruined to lose the enticing sight, he could all at once not bring himself to look anywhere else but her face.

The idea of his atrocious behaviour burned like pitch. *Gods, he'd nearly lost it. Nearly… nearly… nearly!*

Harkubsah's Place

Malandar turned his eye to the large barn directly ahead. The wide-open timber doors lacked varnish and called in silent misery for the benefit of an expert carpenter to fix various discrepancies before they fixed themselves permanently in the ground, yet the sudden whinnying of a horse was for now all that mattered. The common stench of worship seemed to have dried up around here too: perhaps it had shrivelled into the Void, time taking its toll on that as well as everything else in sight, or maybe, this Harkubsah was not as much of an oaf as previously hinted? *It wasn't much, but…*

A fat man appeared, hopping from the darkened insides with a peculiar lilting walk, blinking owlishly as though just awakened from a late nap. Malandar inhaled, and-

And nearly forgot to breathe as he spat the breath back out. *If there'd been no pollution of the air before, then now…*

Abandoning the task of dusting himself off, the First Guardian slowly straightened and gave the man a serene look though he regretted not positioning himself upwind. The horse-coper's eclectic array of bad smells were arriving well before the man himself, and sure – if he might not worship the Mad Ones, then neither did he worship water or soap.

Almost bemused by his apparent run of ill-luck, a sigh escaped Malandar. The man approached with a shrewd smile, wearing a stained greying shirt that had been washed too many times, yet not enough, and a style of greasy back-swept hair which required no oil to fuel a gleam that complimented the sudden beady interest in his dish-water pale eyes. To accredit the lack of style, baggy trousers tugged into wide-shafted boots had been left to sag precariously below an impressive gut - a look which instantly offered the alarming impression that Malandar was in imminent danger of facing a partially-naked hustler.

As he watched the man traipse across the yard at strange leisure, he sincerely hoped such an atrocity wouldn't happen today. *Dear maker…*

"M'lord, welcome!" the man gushed with bombastic enthusiasm when he was still fifteen yards removed, his expression changing to inspire trust though his eyes never once stopped roving. Booming, he added, "Indeed, good eve, good eve! I am Jab Harkubsah, t'owner an' p'prietor here. An' M'lord is?"

Malandar felt derision cipher into his stance but shifted to cover it.

To the First Guardian, there was only one way to interpret the way the man looked at him like he'd come wrapped in gold cloth and had presented Harkubsah with a jade coffer of Dragon Silver. The man saw profit: in any shape, anyhow - and it might not necessarily have to involve the sale of a horse or two. *Lone travellers had accidents…*

Malandar's mood turned a full hundred degrees towards frosty but it seemed not to matter to the fat man. Dust or no, the sorry excuse for a Human had already zoned in on the darkly rich material of the First Guardian's long, narrow-sleeved coat which was Elvern vicuna woven with sea silk and embellished with ebonised-gold stitches of warning and honour: the orthodox sigils - *and some less conventional* - awarded the Weaver of the 7th Tier upon attaining this most cardinal mastery.

Unfortunately, Harkubsah would not recognise the provenance, nor the origins - however, he'd assuredly assume fine cloth and decent tailoring an indication of wealth just the same. A leather satchel could hide a multitude of goods, including monetary riches, and of course, the short internal debate as to whether the Guardian's unadorned belt might merely be polished metal made to look pure Dragon Silver or if it could indeed be

Dragon Silver polished to seem dull metal, had doubtlessly been forded too. *It left only the swords then.* Travellers were wont to know a certain proficiency with the weapons they carried, but skill was relative. *Yes, Malandar knew Harkubsah would be wondering.*

The First Guardian sucked back the urge to draw on the now-limited power of his runes, shifted his weight and folded his arms like it might hold him from Persuading a Weave and releasing a spell that no matter how finely executed, would still reverberate like a chime to raise knowledge of his presence. *It would not do either. He was here for a reason...*

"I need horses;-" he stated with cutting cool and a narrowed-eyed stare that seemed to momentarily stun the man and irreversibly flay the idea from Harkubsah's mind that this new customer harboured any intentions of ever clasping his outstretched hand, "-two or three. Fit. Of brave persuasion, nasty if necessary - I care not what temperament, providing they have proven stamina."

"Ah... eh... well an' good then." The fat man seemed to wilt slightly under the Guardian's direct gaze and he hastily withdrew the grimy hand left floundering in the space between them. It seemed he was taken aback, but not enough to prevent his eyes from fluttering once more from Malandar's satchel, to the belt, to his swords, as he said, "Wud... Wud M'lord care t'come tis way, then?"

Malandar nodded curtly, then followed this Jab Harkubsah, with his terrible accent and even more horrendous stench, to the large barn with the peeling doors. Already he was semi-idly wondering if the halfwit would try and rob him now or at least wait until a more opportune moment? *As it stood, he'd wager good gold it could still go fifty-fifty - now what was it he'd heard several of these Humans say upon hearing of his 'misfortune'? 'Fleck' was it?*

He thought so.

Well, fleck indeed! He really didn't need this. The man's stench would not improve with death!

In spite of the urges fluttering through his mind, Malandar kept his face void of emotion though he already regretted setting eye on the coper. He needed horses, so he stayed, but he didn't appreciate being sized up like one of the animals he was about to inspect, nor did he enjoy the horse-copers gushing, too-familiar tones. He'd dealt with people like that before though: every race had them, and now... magic or no... so it began again!

Inside, the roof skylights were dirty and the barn dark, yet it smelled of clean haylage, warm horse and golden leather oil. As Malandar's eyes quickly adjusted, for a wonder it would appear likely that for now, Jab Harkubsah was honestly intent upon selling him a steed or two, as he went about shouting for his grooms to bring 'the two chestnuts, the two brown and the grey'.

"So 'ow far does M'lord need t' go tis fine eve?" Harkubsah tried his conversational skills again, whilst he stood back to watch the lads spring into action.

"Far," Malandar told him as he ran his eyes around the stables.

In opposition to the derelict feeling bequeathed upon a visitor outside, the inside of Master Harkubsah's enterprise appeared a well-maintained, tightly run affair, with two rows of suitably spacious stalls flanking a wide central corridor. From the size, it might be estimated that Harkubsah owned space for more than two dozen liveries, with more to be added if the fields were employed too, yet from what the first Guardian could glean in the fuzzy, greyscale light, the fat horse-monger was sorely short of stock.

Attention wandering, he followed the progress of the stable hands. Already the first horse was being led forth, the crisp clipped sound of shod hooves calling out in promise of success as the groom passed them with a tall grey mare of a long even stride. *An Arrow... the pale coat and sturdy conformation gave the horse away...*

A slight shuffle next to him brought his attention away from the animal - his passing assessment of the mare now shifting to the repulsive Human once more. Harkubsah was not looking at the horse, nor was he tallying up the chances of his customer making this purchase a surety. Instead, the coper had used the small interlude to sidle closer and his eyes lingered upon the arcane symbols along the back of the First Guardian's right sleeve with the interest of a man already calculating the profit of a rare acquisition.

Malandar resisted the urge to swat the man off his feet like he'd resisted the urge to hunt down the Venzoian presence he'd felt earlier and retreated a step instead. Up close and sheltered, the man reeked stronger than a host of decomposing Hyatt'Raah. From the shifty sheen of speculation in his eyes, it was clear he might suffer similar lack of self-restraint also and when he offered the Guardian a bent servile smile of tobacco-stained teeth, the gall of having had to leave Ambar'Zadron behind blazed through the First Guardian yet again.

"M'lord owns a fine coat," Jab Harkubsah commented, sleekly inquisitive, "but I do no' recognise the codex he wears so unusually displayed. Tell me good Sir, wud this be of Yellow Snake or maybe Tuxaman origins?

"Neither." Malandar shifted as the man made a gesture towards him as though bold enough to touch the sleek fabric uninvited.

Appearing chastised, Harkubsah folded his hands and averted his gaze. "M'lord forgive me that was inappropriate. If I might ask to your name, I might-"

"Not now." Malandar shot at the coper and moved to void himself of the need to break the man's fingers. Harkubsah's presence – and stench - still buzzed at the periphery of his attention, but determined to concentrate on the task at hand, Malandar eyed the next pair of horses as a second lad brought them forth.

Two chestnuts this time, a pleasant-looking mare and a gelding - the latter was of a surprisingly fine quality, but unfortunately also suffering from some sort of injury, which made the dragging of its left hind a surety that the horse was lame.

Without waiting to be invited, Malandar followed the grooms back outside to perform a quick examination of the animals. Of the final two fetched out for inspection by the first lad again, one horse looked a sway-backed nag and the other somehow as careworn as the establishment itself; this would not take long...

None of them were good enough for his purpose. Not by a long twist. He'd also have no magic to spare on enhancing their character either - yet, as the grey snorted and rolled her eyes at him, he knew she might just have enough spirit to see him off for a while at least.

It left only the chestnut mare. Of Kaldun origins, she was smaller than the grey but appeared well-kept and inquisitive, happily stretching towards him as the gentile Kalduns were wont, her pleasant disposition melting into him.

"This is all you have?" Malandar straightened from checking the gelding's dodgy leg.

"M'lord we hav' no' got much goin' tho' these days. It all goes t' Zanzier, I'm told." The vendor shrugged with apology that looked almost genuine. "Yet, if M'lord waits a han'ful o' days, we might get a dozen goin' tho', but-"

"Out of the question, I cannot wait," Malandar cut in and saw the man's eyes glitter with this new nugget of information.

Harkubsah sighed in assimilated sympathy though. "Well, M'lord sure is unfortunate t' find himself wie' no horse, then. It puts a dear strain on everythin', don't it? Such a sad thing, really, but I imagine…

"Well, I imagine M'lord is behin' his business schedule, then?"

Malandar gave him a level stare – *the man could assume what he wanted* - and Jab Harkubsah just about managed to suppress a shrewd smile as he turned to one of the lads, a blond-haired stocky youth with a shovel chin and dark eyes.

"Well M'lord, perhaps m' lad could 'elp?" The coper rubbed his chin, feinting a pensive air of concern, as he carried on, "Tis lad, he knows tis land like t' back o' his hand, he does. He could show M'lord t' quickest route, if M'lord but tells him wher' to?"

The Guardian smiled to himself: a grimace of tired reluctance, really. The man was peering up at him as if he fully expected Malandar to agree to the venture and when the Guardian didn't object, Harkubsah slinked a little close, undoubtedly sensing a steal.

Malandar sighed.

"I will need no 'guide'," he assured the man and the youth, visually assessing the chestnut mare one final time, though his mind was already made up.

"Ah then, very well. Tis M'lord's choice o' course." Shrugging with too much emphasis on disregard, the horse dealer's tongue flickered across pudgy lips as he favoured the Guardian a smirk, "An' t' horses, then?"

Malandar quirked an eyebrow but relented. *The fat man was like a bad shadow. One way or another this scum would rob him today: what he would pay for a beast here would probably be twice the price of an Afhpar pure-blood in the old days. Pity...*

"I will take the grey and the chestnut mare," he told Harkubsah. "I assume you have tack?"

The man looked crestfallen. "Ah... M'lord... t' mi grief I wud hav' t' charge separate for t' tack. I'm 'fraid times are hard an'-"

"I will pay for the tack," Malandar bit out, finally meeting the Vendor's eyes and forcing the man to hold his gaze a blink longer than necessary, as he continued, "And I will pay for the two mares specified. Name your price, but do not take me for a fool."

The horse-coper relaxed with an affable smile. "For you M'lord, Ghost the grey be one n'alf gold plate includin' tack. She's part Arrow-blood, you kno' and I don't see her go f'less. The chestnut gelding wud b' cheaper, M'lord, but t'lady stepper will cost you an additional fifty gold and a quarter silver. Tis a fair price, as it stands tis day, M'lord. A fair price."

For a wonder, Malandar agreed. *The man had given him a fair price indeed - only a little over what he'd expected.* It instantly raised suspicions. And yet he had to go with it.

Aware of the moment the coper's gaze flashed across his belt yet again, Malandar said, "Then we are in accord. Make them ready, and make swift. I shall pay you upon final inspection."

Jab Harkubsah's grin turned wide. For a blink, he almost reminded the First Guardian of a Hyatt'Raah again, but then he turned to the two hands, shattering the illusion as he barked, "Krit! Demrah! You hear't'Lord! See t'his demand! We wouldn't wanna keep 'im! Demlir, boy, get rid o' t' others!"

Malandar watched the youths jump to comply, one lad quickly separating the two mares to fasten their lead ropes to a pair of iron rings attached to the outside of the barn, the other groom meanwhile handing the rejected horses to a skinny boy who'd appeared from the barn as though shot from a bow. Then the two older boys disappeared too, presumably to fetch harness and saddles.

In the following brief absence of activity, the quiet evening took over. Had the fat, slovenly man not been there it would have felt peaceful - however, had Malandar been riding Zah he would have felt better still! *It was frustratingly obvious.* The horses would break under pace and strain. He would not have time to consider their welfare, and when they went he'd be back to this point again; and again, until-

"M'lord, I'plaud your choice," the coper cut into his revenue, "Indeed, Ghost's a'fine animal that one, oh yes, she's! She's as steady as t'come and she'll run f'leagues wi'out tirin', that I can guarantee. Still, t' make no mistake wi t'other one: she'll serve M'lord well too."

"Oh I'm sure," Malandar replied non-committed, sliding away a step to match the other man's attempt at sideling closer and thus again preventing him from touching the fabric of the desired coat.

"Maybe you would check on the hands' progress," he demanded and did not pause for a reply, before turning his back on the greasy horse dealer to stride briskly across the broken courtyard.

It seemed to do the trick, for Malandar felt the man withdraw finally.

The relief was selfish, yet enjoying the burst of fresh air, he rested both elbows casually across the top rail of the corral, gaze ambling towards the vista of the soon-disappearing sun.

It was drawing late. Somehow, the hour of the quiet prayers was well-progressed and sundown would soon draw darkness. On horseback he would have to be careful if travelling through the night: one small misstep and a horse would be rendered useless, yet would he be forced to outrace a pack of Harkubsah's cronies?

A silent breath escaped him as he was left wondering if Harkubsah was busy organising his moves to relieve his lone customer of all his valuables, perhaps even his life? He expected the canny man would already have 'help' organised for such a task – perhaps even in the form of a gang that – when given a signal - would accost the victim a few miles from here.

Malandar rubbed his brow between thumb and forefinger, unconcerned but frustrated. Without the magic surrounding him, he felt ever-weak. He was not of course, but still. *Did he really look that travel-worn that Harkubsah thought him easy for the taking? Did the fat man perhaps imagine the weapons a pair of display-pieces only - or did he simply think to take the chance that his affluent customer might prove unable to wield them with any particular skill in the face of a surprise attack?*

It was a wager few people would enter into, but perhaps they'd simply shoot him in the back – it would ruin the coat, of course, but hex…

No matter what, the First Guardian did not want to be detained on the road, or worse: risk the horses, and void of excitement, he acceded that this was something he would have to take care of.

It turned his musings grim.

If the Natural Magic hadn't been ripped and warped, the Human would have instantly known not to insult his customer; greed or no, he would've instantly recognised the Runes of Power scored across Malandar's left hand and across his temples, because as First Guardian he would have needed no illusion to hide them!

Sadly, however, Harkubsah did not understand; he did not even recognise the coat of a 7th Tier Spell-Weaver on mere sight either; regretfully, the time where the sigils alone would have acted a repellent were long gone, as was the respect that Harkubsah would have naturally harboured and nurtured for fear of the consequences if he did not.

The Magic lay in ruins - Malandar supposed it had rendered the stitching on his coat little more than rich adornment to the ignorant people of these lands – and now…

He drew in another breath, contemplating options. In actual fact, he had no deep emotions about the horse-coper's little extra-curricular business other than the inconvenience he faced. Some people were scum – magic or no: always had been, always would be. *The lack of respect though…*

A noise brought him back. Slowly he turned to watch the two older lads bring his horses across. It was the same two lads as before. *Krit and Demrah.*

As he'd anticipated, Harkubsah came right in their wake, his odours now partially, but mercifully, masked by the far more agreeable scent of warm horse flesh.

I could kill them all, he thought with sublime matter-of-fact composure, eyes and mind weighing - but of course, a few looks did not make a man guilty, and though he might harbour suspicions, he still could not know if the youths were innocent in this setup, and that…

Killing people carried consequences. Consequences he was not prepared to suffer on behalf of a few half-wits, whom - under normal circumstances - did not warrant a second thought, so… something else then?

Oblivious to his sinister thoughts, the lads steered the mares across to the next section of the corral, tying the reins around the tops of the splintered posts that looked as though locust had chewed on the edges, then went about seeing to the appropriate adjustments of harnesses and saddles. *He could not kill them indiscriminately, no - but there were other choices...*

Observing their work, Malandar went to stroke the pale star on the chestnut Kaldun's forehead. In the budding, purpled-edged twilight, she looked half-decent. Now with the added bonus of having been under the skilful ministration of a decent farrier recently, he supposed she would do as well as needed, at least for a short distance - yet unsurprisingly it was the grey that captured his attention as she sidestepped with a snort, hustling the groom. Named 'Ghost', presumably because of her silvery white coat, she looked in better shape than the chestnut, but then again - it *was* the more valuable of the two, and Harkubsah, despite his faults, had most assuredly protected his best asset accordingly.

Malandar stepped aside to allow the grooms to retreat, but his eyes stayed with Harkubsah as the other man dismissed the lads with a few gruff commands and a clip around the ear for the last one, too slow to move from his path. Then he stepped into the space they'd occupied, slowly busying himself as though to scrutinise the worth of their work.

With a selection of grunts, the coper took his time - and wishing that he could retreat, yet just not trusting the man not to include some last-moment tampering with the tack, Malandar remained closer than choice warranted, ostentatiously putting up with the mixed stench of sour sweat and ale. It was still brilliantly complimented with something that could have rivalled death, but he was beginning to suspect it might be some kind of strong 'slave' tobacco instead.

The latter gave insight. *The grey leaves might stink to the Boundary and back but they were not cheap; if the horse vendor was a 'slave' addict his dishonesty might be understood, if not condoned.* It also meant that the man must be relatively successful at this side-line business too – otherwise he could not have afforded the smoke.

Malandar frowned.

"So m'gracious Lord has a hurry for a reason?" The Vendor looked up from fussing with the chestnut's nose straps to find Malandar's gaze fixed on him. "I mean… I just imagine wi'out a horse, tis been 'ard travelling, eh?"

Malandar simply looked at the man.

"You assume correct," he deigned to concur after a blink, then added, "Will this take all night?"

"No M'lord, jus' a few moments now." The man bobbed his head as though in apology, moving quickly from the chestnut to the grey. Pulling at a chinstrap, then loosening the buckle one notch, he offered Malandar a sideways glance, "If M'lord travels out tonight I shall offer up suitable prayers to safeguard his journey. The moon might b' out, but tis not yet full; horses hav' been known t' stumble on poorer roads, I believe."

Malandar looked away with a fey smile. "Your concern is noted. I guarantee I will be careful."

"I'm relieved then, M'lord.-" The First Guardian could hear the smirk in the coper's voice. "-M'lord is no' from roun' here – that is, judgin' by what he wears an' all – so allow me to recommend the northerly path? It appears to steer back east but only for a league and it catches the main trail, cutting the route by a good three leagues."

It was a casually innocent suggestion; helpful even. Taking the woodland path would bring a traveller across the ground with speed, but once beneath the looming shadows of those pines…

Malandar almost sighed. Again. *Inkar'Chi be hanged: if you wanted to rob somebody then a little more subtlety might be in order, but maybe these times were a lot different in that respect too!*

"I shall consider the suggestion," Malandar said and felt how Harkubsah paused the already slow job of cinching a saddle strap to eye *M'lord* with a speculative frown for the smooth hilts of the gently curving twin swords harnessed to his back. *Hope still lived that the man would choose wisely, but barely.*

Turning back to his work with one last lingering look for Malandar's swords, the coper tucked down on a stirrup strap, securing the item with speedy habit, and with a sixth sense that never failed, the Guardian knew then that the repulsive dung-brain was done calculating. The man reeked of more than 'slave' and dusty sweat now; this - well, if Malandar was not wrong - *and he rarely was* - this would not be a decision that would act in the man's favour after all.

"Lady of my heart, we..." Bilan's voice shook, efforts to keep buried the self-loathing thoroughly compromising his strength of conviction, "...we must not do this."

Attempting not to notice Iambre's hunted eyes boring into his, he looked at the floor with an agonised frown.

Quickly, before the words became trapped in his throat, he said, "Milady, we cannot do this. It is not right and as I live to protect you, I cannot dishonour you in such a way."

He hacked down a breath, something in his chest sawing; ripping. Speaking the necessary words were harder than voicing a battlefield charge-command, yet he'd rallied, and whilst the meaning of his 'attack' hit her, he sidestepped her presence with a rapid sideways glance, thinking to give her space to straighten out.

Still, a thing that could not be side-stepped was his lingering, aching regret.

The sentiment tugged at his reserves. A beast of old - relegated to the prison he'd once erected on the inside, but still screaming and clawing at every fibre of his body now – seemed to curse and taunt his weakness, daring him to change his mind; daring him to take what was offered!

It was little more than a wistful fantasy, though. A good past, was a silent past. He could not add this smear to what he'd already exorcised and expect a continued reprieve. No-

Breathing deeply, he tried to trash a new wave of contradictory feelings. *He did not trust himself enough to remain in control. He was weak, and if she was mad enough to reach out for him now, he'd be lost.*

He needn't have worried though. Rooted to the spot, he watched numbly as Iambre moved, skirting as though stepping on broken glass to pass beyond his ability to reach both physically, and mentally.

It demoted him to little better than that of an ill-received visitor or trespassing madman, and though the Captain thought her wise, he could find no honesty within to replace regret that she did not hide her true feelings as she straightened her skirts with a sideways tug.

Sighting him with a gelid stare down her nose, the Princess managed to sink back her shoulders to gain inches in stature before allocating a moment to smooth down errant locks of hair with such delicate deliberate care not to dislodge the golden amber-inlaid pins.

He should rejoice. The chill that seemed to rise like a wall of air between them was more than just a fancy impression. *Icy scorn. Just for him. Because of him. It ought to fill him with the hearty cheer of success, yet-*

Unsettled by the very shift he'd prayed for, he dropped his gaze again. The warm memory of her silken hair in his face had him wishing he could turn back time as his treacherous imagination would not quite stop at the same point his physical counterpart had managed. *But the ice was in the way now.*

With a guarded sigh he banished the images, mentally shredding any lingering ideas, focusing instead on the state of his own clothes to bring the uniform back into a semblance of order.

Blood and ashes - and it was a good thing too - before Palea returned, or the Banquet Master arrived, or the Viper...

Smoothing palms down his pristine white shirt with a rushed move, Bilan tucked one side back behind the waistband of his black breeches and was conveniently forced to schedule his eyes to the task of navigating belts and layers, to re-tie strings and straighten the leather straps of his green uniform doublet.

It gave familiar purpose. Somewhere along their tryst, Iambre's plundering hands had managed to skewer the presentation and it was not acceptable for any member of the Legion to ignore smart appearances when attired in official court uniform. For a fact, news travelled fast, and he could hardly expect the men to follow dress code if he himself did not see fit to do so - *never mind, what they might make of where and when he'd been at the time of neglect!*

Sufficiently sobered now, Bilan focused on his task, the awkward silence stretching like a decomposing hide between them, threatening to tear the future in half at any undue moment unless they both managed to adhere to the rules.

Of course, he knew that he should apologise again for his shameful conduct. Even if they pretended at love, he should have more restraint than what a few kisses could undo in a matter of heartbeats. It didn't even matter, that in his defence, he had a hard time determining right from wrong when it came to matters of Iambre; it didn't matter that his mind somehow continued to cloud until even the most clear-set laws seemed blurred beyond good health and self-preservation. *They both stood to lose too much! Both knew the fancy of allure would never be enough!*

Bilan ate another onslaught of regret the way he might have twisted to shoulder a glancing dagger blow to the clavicle, rather than accept a killing blow full to the chest. It hurt like the fabled bite of Osari'Chi's mother-spitting-foaming-at-the-jaws-Sa'brans, but at least he'd live. *At least...*

Gathering will, he steeled resolve: he'd formally apologise, then he'd get her another member of his unit to act as escort - that would be a start – and then-

Looking directly at Iambre, the quickly prepared words arrested on his tongue. *The ice had melted before the fire she was stroking, and her eyes now gleamed as though the amber had been turned liquid.* An apology would infuriate her, he suspected. It would smear the 'incident' as something less, and it hadn't been. *Gods' curses; he should have saddled that flecking horse...*

Hoping she'd dismiss him from sight, he waited for her to speak, and found himself the sudden victim of a silent prayer, she would not do so after all. Together they had never felt so delicate: so much like strangers, but she was slowly winning back control of herself and when she did...

"Captain, you are a brave man indeed and I must commend you on your level of self-control." Looking at a spot past his right shoulder, Iambre drew a hand past the hairline at her ear, using the edge of her little finger to direct an already perfectly arrayed strand of hair back into alignment, as she continued, "So evidently your head continues to fight your heart, and my…" She paused with a soft derisive snort, then said, "Well mercy, what fortuitous luck for the both of us, yet dear Gods, how I wish-"

With a shrug of feinted indifference, she cut herself off, the would-be wish replaced by a sarcastic twist of the mouth that conveyed equal measures mockery and embarrassment. On what appeared to be an incidental whim, she offered him a long look then: something of searching weight and cruel brevity.

Yet before he'd felt the full weight of that look, a shiver shrivelled her stance, and she turned from him instead, needlessly checking skirts and jewellery, though just like the hair, she no longer displayed a ribbon out of place.

"Oh but I should think that a lesser man would not have managed to restrain himself with thus unerring strength of persuasion,-" she shot at him, a new terrible note of self-mockery coiling in and round every syllable, as she needlessly picked at the fabric around the filigree belt, "-and Gods know we might have landed ourselves in much trouble, so for your clear thinking, I am no doubt in your debt."

Silent frustration brimming, Bilan raked a hand through his hair. He could hear the anger now; it showed in the strain of her shoulders, in the way she held her head, in the way the timbre of her voice turned, and he braced like a jouster about to meet the opponent's lance, hopefully with enough strength and skill to preserve himself from being unhorsed by superior technique.

She huffed under her breath, and ironically it occurred to him that she'd already thrown him in the dirt and would no longer offer him grace to yield, but he kept the notion to himself as she moved back to her former seat to stand behind the tall frame as though in search of support and shield.

Placing hands too privileged for cracked skin or dirty fingernails atop of the chest-high back rail, she paused a beat, gathering composure as though about to make a public declaration before the Senate – and yet for her clever front, from the way she clutched the upholstery she'd already given her emotions away before she finally looked him in the eye again. *And yes indeed: there was the anger of a princess scorned, her wrath stemmed only by the woman with broken dreams.*

"Yes, I believe I am in your debt,-" she reiterated sharply as she drew the long breath of someone tired of fighting, "-and so, a warning would serve, Captain. A final warning. You see, I would sincerely advise that you never again feel inclined to see it as your responsibility to convince me that I am some budding victim!

"Gods, but would it not be a lie to pretend that I did not just want to follow you down the path we so nearly engaged upon? Would it not?!"

A sad, regretful smile flashed across her face as her fingers seemed to knead the armchair's padded back independent of conscious thought, and yet again Bilan wondered if something else was also the matter, but then her words seemed to belie the notion.

"I would have cherished this, Bilan." For a blink the corners of her eyes crinkled. "In the months and years to come, I would have guarded the memory like a jealous Dragon atop a towering mountain of treasure. *That is what we are. That is what you are. To me!* I hope… well, I hope that you understand this."

Staring into eyes made of honeyed steel, Bilan felt a hot twinge. But, even if he wanted nothing better than to oblige her, he could not possibly offer her any hope and still perform his official role. It would simply be too hard. All he could promise was to complete his sworn duty – nothing more; not if either of them ever wanted peace of mind again.

"Your Highness, if there were a way to make you mine…" Words faltering at her blank expression, Bilan tried again, "You know that I will always fight for you; that I will always be your man in every proper sense of the word, but-

"Ah Gods, I must be true to my duty, to your duty, or… or we will both be damned."

"And so I shall send you home?" she challenged in obvious frustration, fingers going pale from the strain of clawing the wine-embroidered cloth as though she sought to strangle the pattern of the weave from existence.

"Milady, I shall stay or go as you wish," he told her, clasping at straws to please her, "but any moment now, the Banquet Master will call on you to attend. This is what you must focus on now. Anything beyond that is not important now."

Appealing to all her good senses of logic and duty, Bilan held her gaze a beat longer than necessary, then drew her attention to the bedroom doors with a sideways glance and a curt nod. In hushed tones, he said, "Gods, we could have been found out and that would have been sure disaster. Here is not the time or the place for... well, you know..."

Iambre's full lips drew apart, warping to match the storm of sweet contempt in her eyes.

Faltering, Bilan met her assumed taunt with a frown of consternation, then he took the righteous approach. "Milady may disagree, of course, but... well, rightly Milady, nowhere should be such a place - and we both know it!"

The princess trapped her bottom lip with her front teeth, pulling her features slightly askew as her face soured. *This was not going right; for one, this was not quite what he had wanted to say. The woman had luminous eyes, but tonight the liquid stare held the heat to scorch suns...*

Bilan Metavo drew a hand over his face, exasperated.

"You know Captain-" Iambre spoke with a commanding edge now. "-I do of course not make light habit of the type of folly you and I appear engaged in - and yet you presume to lecture me on matters of conduct; on issues I am already too crucially aware of! Mercy, did I not just tell you that I love you? Am I not the flecking Crown Princess - who might damned-well do what, and as, she pleases?"

Ever-shocked by her swearing, Bilan ignored the trap, nodded, and Iambre's eyes narrowed to flecks of amber that could have belonged to a feline protecting its territory.

"Good then!" Sounding vindicated, she flicked her chin at him. "You see, if I want to throw away my 'honour' then it is my call, do you hear! My call!"

Bilan's deepening consternation pulled his eyebrows high and the double frown-line higher yet.

That reached her somehow. In a flash she appeared to lose the steel in her spine and attitude, folding suddenly into someone more tractable; more vulnerable in her honesty.

Swallowing hard, she licked her lips. "Dear Gods Bilan, if not for you, do you think that I would play with the reputation of my House? With the future of our realm? Do you think I would just have a little racy fun with the common captain of my guard? Bilan, I am not a flirt, nor am I a child! Don't you think that I understand exactly what I ask of you? That I do not see what consequences it might have?!"

For a moment Iambre's face dropped with the plea and purpose of her thoughts, and when he said nothing she issued a venomous snort. "Gods Bilandro! For all I care the whole ruddy banquet can wait if I deem it so necessary - because I will not let your pig-headed notions of honour and righteousness ruin our chances of having something real together, do you hear?!"

At this point, Bilan knew he wanted to say something right and poignant, yet nothing sprung to mind, and Iambre gestured in appeal, voice going soft, "You are a man. I am a woman. You desire me, do you not?"

She leaned forward, her hair swaying like heavy waves etched in white-blonde gold. With a gesture of appeal she muttered, "Black rats, I am surely not asking for anything you wouldn't do in a heartbeat if matters were just a little different – if… if I were just a common tavern wench! Bilan, my love, I… I know that I cannot keep you, but don't you see that I would? In a heartbeat, I would. If I could."

Breathing deeply, she suddenly seemed aware of her clutching hold of the chair and let go as if stung.

Bilan, in turn, was speechless. The sum of her words was not the distancing talk that he'd anticipated but rather a finely-woven counterattack. *What could his answer possibly be? What could he possibly respond with, or say, that was not an outright lie? If she had been any other woman, he'd have-*

He shook his head in denial. *No, no, no…*

"Crown Princess, I-"

"We do not stand on parade," her blunt interruption cut off his faltering words, "I have a name! Use it or insult me!"

"Lady Iambre, I am… I am beyond words. You say 'take me', when yet you know that I can never keep you! Do you enjoy this cruelty? Is that it?" Bilan forced down a breath, but it did not seem to alleviate the stress in his chest. "Milady, you must know that when my service to you is ended, I will never again find peace if I have called you 'mine' and 'lover' – perhaps not ever, regardless!"

Iambre opened her mouth to argue, then held herself back on a breath as her eyes clouded with new consideration, the flaming amber growing tepid as the insight of his revelation slowly settled. Without a doubt she was searching for a solution, but…

With poorly disguised bitterness, Bilan shook his head, stalling further argument. "No Milady, please… no. Better then to hold fast and avoid the heartache that must otherwise come to both of us. Better then to hold fast!"

The 'clouds' deepened. Iambre wet her lips. He sensed her frustration like a strangeness in the air before an ambush, and feeling the fight suddenly leave his heart, he heaved a small sigh.

Raising his hands in a gesture to disarm, he said, "Lady Iambre, please understand, I beg of you. You... you affect me so that I can barely keep my wits about me; if you... if you do not agree to be strong about this, it will not only ruin you, it will cripple me also."

And there it was – the entire truth of it all. She would of course already know this, but now he'd said it aloud for the both of them to hear and watching for any sign of acknowledgement, he slowly lowered his hands, not daring to move any other part. The way he felt about her meant that he would not want her, not even for a brief time when ultimately he'd have to let her go. The future would be gloomy enough even without *that kind* of memory to sustain him and try as he like to twist his desire into something sullied and black, he knew that he would never be able to consider her in the simple, belittling terms of a golden conquest. *He'd not be a man if he wasn't sorely tempted of course - but he was better than that now.*

His lips twitched with a sick smile. Iambre looked decidedly ill too as she struggled to speak whatever was on her mind, and he eyed the water clock on the mantelpiece - a huge silver thing covered in stylised lily pads, unknown birds and what appeared to be a leaping eagle.

Regret was useless. Any moment the call for banquet would come and with that, Palea and Gods knew who else, would appear. He had to keep his tenuous hold on composure. *Had to!*

Several drops of water fell as the silence grew drab once more and Iambre abandoned speech in favour of working her skills to transform her face back to a mask of carefully mastered serenity, but another tired sigh escaped her, and Bilan had never before heard such resignation in such a small sound. *Mercy...*

"Oh my love, you leave me little choice!" she mumbled at length, the cast of her eyes growing mildly haunted as she favoured him a pained look of reluctant capitulation. "But Gods... I have much regard for you... and you are most certainly determined in this, so... well, my... what lady would not love you doubly for your loyalty? Indeed Bilan, I certainly do not wish to be angered by this; truly I do not, but we should be one!"

With the words came a strange aching relief, yet her simple candour also cut him like the finest Dragon Silver: true to the heart.

Iambre looked at the wall, her face haunted by another bittersweet smile, as though for a moment she appeared to be thinking of something else.

Then offering the wall a small nod of accord, quite like they'd just shared a silent communiqué, she said, "Very well then Bilan. After Zanzier I will grant you the peace you seek: I shall have your decommission documents drafted and ready for my signature – along with a suitable letter of merit and full honours for your service, of course. My father will not fault a thing. In fact, in my view, he should offer you another promotion."

Iambre drew a shuddering breath and trailed her eyes slowly back to his. It seemed something was dragging at her attention though, for it was the longest, slightest movement Bilan had ever endured to watch. *Her capitulation made him numb from the spine out. It was for the best, truly it was, but-*

Iambre smiled her sad smile, looked away, and he knew an odd sense of despair.

The bizarre twist of life wasn't lost on him. He was a confident man, respected, well-liked even if his position within the Legion afforded considerable rank and power anyway; for a Commoner, he had done very well - and that in spite of his age. *Why must he go tangle with the stars where he'd never belong? Who in their right mind did that?*

Bilan clenched his fists as he tried to wipe his mind clear of a sudden, unbidden picture of Iambre with her future husband. *He had not the right! No right at all, and still! He might have saved one King, but there were no guarantees he might not as easily assassinate another…*

A deadly quiet filled the reception room, only the occasional crack of burning logs and flights of the rising sparks breaking the stillness. He looked at Iambre, but absently toying with her usual strand of hair she'd blocked him in favour of a distant, extrovert expression. *It should have felt peaceful, serene even, but of course-*

The three short, official-sounding raps on the main doors broke the odd atmosphere, but though expected, Bilan reflexively straightened with a jolt, even as Iambre shot away from the chair, simultaneously smoothing the front of her shimmering skirt.

Instinctively locking eyes, they shared a heartbeat of unvoiced understanding, even as the short slender Palea glided from the dressing room to allow entry a short-legged middle-aged man with a seven-foot bronze staff crowned by a monstrous eagle-head that seemed to preside like some stern, belittling judge above them all.

Bilan hid a frown. The rich blue fabric of the servant's robes could not hide the Master of Banquets' striking resemblance to a wind-dried prune - however, as he viewed it, the man could've been decked in horse manure, for Palea would've made him welcome regardless with her graceful curtsies and studied poise. *She too had come along way, since Iambre scooped her from that temple; why could he not have loved-*

He shook himself angrily and focused on the prune as he approached, too slow for patience, yet too formally correct not to spell 'etiquette' with every humble step. With a hunched-over carriage and the ruddy-beaked face of a man who likes his port a little too much and should undoubtedly follow hedge-doctor advice to heed concerns about the gout currently gnawing at his health, the Master of *pomp* looked ailing, and Bilan was inspired to see past the 'prune' to the invisible 'vultures' circling a walking dead man.

Though not amused, he smiled to himself - a rapid grimace - as the Master of Ceremonies came to a stop, bashed his staff into the ground to set the floor-bound silver candelabras shivering, then intoned, "Oh sorely have we awaited this joy. Oh worried from woe and strain, did we eagerly await her precious Highness's safe arrival in this most humble of ancient provinces. Now glad are our hearts, therefore; outmost inspired do I feel in the pleasure to stand before Your Grace in order to convey, that the Knights Commander of the West most graciously bids the Lady Crown Princess come join him at the welcoming banquet in Her honour. Pleasing Her Grace: there will be much to enjoy. Pleasing Her Grace, I shall now guide her on the route I myself in humble obedience find the most interesting."

Bowing from the waist, the desiccated little man offered Iambre grace with well-honed precision, awaiting without a falter, for her leave to straighten.

He was so official that she should not have been offended in any way, and yet Bilan saw a tightness in her smile that usually denoted ill-approval. It was gone in a blink, and as expected she inclined her chin towards the officious man, "It pleases me, so I will attend."

84

Without a sound to signal approval, the Master of Banquets bowed momentarily lower, but somehow managed to appear vindicated by his own importance also.

That was no mean feat. Bilan shot the man a bland look. The further west they travelled, the less he liked the people, but at least he was fairly certain that pumped up by his own importance, the prune would lead them the long way to banquet – so perhaps that was one good thing - Gods' rot, but then again…

More time with Iambre was maybe the last thing he needed now!

Solancei's Memoirs

The Province of Tarléon.
Ocean's End.
Autumn of 780 P. C. W.

Yes, so I feared for Rainan: that could not be helped. Yet the gentle tinkle of bells within the horses' tails soon soothed me almost as effectively as the Veranto had done. *It would be all right. Ivanor was just beyond the horizon. Soon we would see the north tower. Soon.*

Like a black-charred arm bursting from the ground, pointing one slender finger straight to the heavens as if to smell the direction of the next weather-break, Fjeldarah's tower would be the first feature to show us the way. *As it had done so many others before, and would continue to do for many more in the future too: providing a haven...*

Of course, that is my crooked fondness of the place glossing over the truth now, for in reality it could never be said that Ivanor was less than a dark, strategic monster of draconian properties, but I still forget sometimes.

Indeed, in reality, my parents' fortress was not, nor will it ever be, 'charming' like the Earl of Elarion's dusty pink estate, Abodenrah, nor does it possess Servangar's flowing poetry of architecture – but still, to me, it was home just the same! *Home and safety. Something to cling to; an illusion...*

And so here, I will pause just a blink. For perspective, if you will.

As you have undoubtedly understood by now, the Province of Tarléon was, and still is, unforgiving. If you ever see it, and I suppose you might one day – would you question my fondness of such a place, I wonder? Will you even care?

Oh but see, I hope you will care - if not for the place, then at least for the sentiment I seek to instil, so that you will recognise what it means to know your 'home' - and then to embrace the knowledge that you may not get to keep it.

Because the importance of 'home' cannot, and should not, be underestimated; wherever you are, I pray you remember this, but 'home' is so much simpler than some might tell you. See, I lived for many years in Servangar, and it was a fine gem to call 'home' too - yet for all that I loved it there, my heart was still east though I was not. The distance, the loss of it, always burned me, but I should not have allowed it to do so. Home is where your love is, but I did not know; did not recognise this, so now I pray to the Maker that you will.

For you it will be something different, but to this day, for me, the barren, clean beauty of Tarléon still cannot be compared. It is a beauty which prevails even when out on the Grave Ice; a beauty, which - once in Servangar - I often longed to set eye upon again, if only to re-affirm the pictures in my mind, and the memories in my heart. However, memories and feelings often confuse each other to meet somewhere beyond the truth - so find home; find peace; then carry it with you wherever you go so that you will not know the same disappointment as I.

Because sadly, it would be a goodly long while before my long-standing wish to see Ivanor was finally granted, and by then…

As it happened, the first time I returned home, I had just turned twenty-three. I was ecstatic, yet rather than bringing me the expected joy, it made me feel hollow in a way that brought to life Taliana's loss and the death of my parents as if it had happened only yesterday. Also, it was not the homecoming I would have chosen for obvious reasons, yet in the end, I was glad, for I went there as part of the Crown Princess' grand tour of Ostravah: it was busy and madness through and through, but it distracted from the fact that I did not enjoy the stay as I imagined I should have: the place was darker; different; colder; not home… *not home at all.*

And then, as for the second time…

Well, the second time I went there on my own, for reasons I could not have predicted, with an outcome that now haunts me for the bargain made across the ice, and for that I am sorry. *Selfishly sorry.*

I find peace in the rare moments, but I think I have lost the idea of 'home' now. Whatever the substitutes I once made, they have gone too – swept away, or re-ordered into something different that is not quite the same as what it once was. Too much has happened, and much will yet come to pass, but I want to implore you with whatever right I might have: if you have the feeling of home in your heart, never jeopardise it! It will remain a constant and lend you strength wherever you go, whatever you do, and to lose it...

Oh but anyway... I imagine I have no right to offer advice and I should not digress. We are still with the seven-year-old me, and I cared not for the beauty of any landscape at that age, nor for the loss of a dream called 'home'. Crusty edges of glitter and crystalline white, the surroundings flowed past our sledge in synchronised harmony and desolate continuity: my province's fine canvas of harsh light and coldest death – all-in-all fitting, yet utterly uninteresting!

Perchance this was why my head went funny again? Exhaustion and monotony will floor even the stoutest of minds, so maybe? Maybe...

Solancei

A Scent of Something Old – And of Something New

Harkubsah was a half-wit!

For a beat, derision had Malandar by the jugular: in itself a thing of nuisance.

Schooling himself to patience, he let go and forced his lips to bend into a thin smile instead. *And why not? You could not fight the way of the Realm. Not like this.*

He had to remember that Harkubsah was not all at fault. He had to remember that it ultimately stemmed from the cursed meddling of the abominations everyone seemed all-too-keen to name 'Gods' - but curse them all - he had no time for this!

Returning the traveller a smile, the fat man patted the mare's flank as he straightened. "Well, all's nearly ready f'you M'lord."

Bowing, although without much deference, the man made as if to step back to give his customer space to ready payment, but Malandar caught and held the fat vendor's gaze before he could turn away.

"My good fellow," he began, the tone almost affable, "A moment if you would? Before I offer up payment?"

The horse-coper tried to look away but it seemed he couldn't quite manage the feat as the Guardian beheld him with penetrating demand, his eyes of borrowed brown glinting to rival the obsidian sheen of the sheaths protecting the twin swords.

Uneasy, Harkubsah frowned, perhaps sensing something wrong, though he wouldn't be able to pinpoint what.

"Firstly, there is something I would tell you,-" As expected, the man went to speak, but no longer affable, Malandar overruled his efforts, continuing, "-a warning, you might name it? See, although the Maker knows you do not merit the courtesy, I will insist that you listen."

Harkubsah looked nonplussed. "But-"

Malandar shushed him, "No truly you should heed this now, Jab Harkubsah. You see: a thousand-year-old war is about to descend upon these lands and when it does you will have small time to determine what you wish to stand for: Chaos or Alérathnar. I can see which side you will be inclined to show loyalty, but you might wish to reconsider, or else you stand to force my hand most awkwardly - in which case the money I'm about to pay will never hold any value, for your life will be forfeit."

Speaking in a near dispassionate voice as though he was simply reaming off a set of rules from the pages of a book, Malandar's caution lacked all emotion. Whilst he spoke though, Jab Harkubsah had started shaking his head, a wizened smile flickering back to life, clearly to 'assure' Malandar that he did not know what this was all about and that he just intended to do his job here, but the sudden sincerity did not strike true.

Again the man started to speak, and again the First Guardian allowed him no say.

"I am just trying to get to where I need to be before this conflict explodes back to life, you understand," he overruled with silvery cool. "I am in a hurry, yes - extremely low on compassion and certainly fresh out of humouring those who would delay my process. So, with this in mind, I recommend you do not insult me further with your lacking respect and ill-conceived thoughts on how best to steal the possessions off my back!"

By now the fat man was shivering, his head shifting in profuse denial that he had any such intentions. Stammering, he attempted to nail down his innocence, "But M'lord, I wud never, ever-"

"But I think that you would!" Malandar laughed without warmth. "However, your premature death will not serve much: soon there will be enough of that to choke everyone, so I will give you this one opportunity to go back to your stables. Go back: see to your horses, yell at your help, keep your petty schemes alive for a while longer, whatever, but do not meddle with me."

In answer, Jab Harkubsah gave him weak smile. Swallowing and taking a disarming step backwards, he said, "M'lord, I... I'm not sure that you... that you...

"Anyway yes, sure wha'ever you want."

The horse-coper withdrew another step, as though he was not quite certain now about the mental health of this person before him, and Malandar felt a surge of irrational irritation wash over him. Perhaps because it hit him at that precise moment; perhaps because of all the imbalances he'd encountered since his coming here; perhaps just because he was forced to creep around like a piece of vermin to avoid premature detection – *again, he could not have said* - but he was suddenly filled with an unexpected and equally dysfunctional need to give in to a base streak of sinister conduct.

He shouldn't have to lower himself to this kind of behaviour just to gain a little respect from a second-grade citizen. He had no lingering interest in killing the man and he should exercise more care, but suddenly it meant nothing who might see: a simple, quick glimpse of the actual truth would do the trick and the man had offered him his name, so-

The First Guardian had moved to stir the Power tied into his cloak of illusion before he truly realised he was about to. It was not linked to the magic of the Realms but to the Maker Himself and thus the reserve rolled to obey his demand without a hint of the surrounding irregularity.

It was a small thing, it barely gave off a hint of magic, but it immobilised the vendor: binding the man to the ground and Malandar proceeded to flex the spell of his guise with just enough subtlety to further the understanding between them.

It took less than a heartbeat – yet the result was most gratifying. For a single moment, the horse-coper looked up at the First Guardian's face with an incredulous frown, then shock peeled across his features as something forgotten appeared to click into place.

Harkubsah's jaw dropped… *like a slack-wit*… and Malandar saw the man remember *something* then.

"Oh… M'lord…" the man whimpered, swaying on his feet, "M'lord I-"

"No, do not waste words," Malandar told the Human as the man 'heeled' like a corpse to the call of a chanting necromancer.

Showing his true colours to just anybody was not a habit he intended to take up, but the moment he saw his petty revelation take a hold, Malandar knew there would be no further trouble from Harkubsah. Whatever the man had been intending or planning, it was forgotten now; drained or burned from his spirit at the instant he'd gleaned the truth about the traveller. *And yet…*

With a lingering drop of contempt for the man, Malandar flexed the fingers on his left hand minutely to freeze time. *Except, that he didn't. Not really.*

Not only was such a spell not allowed, it was also taxing beyond compare, and a Weaver - *even one of the 7th Tier* - would need full dispensation to perform any such altercation or the punishment was capital. It was of course now rather a thing of irrelevance too, for even if he'd been bent on using illegal Weaves, the current state of magic would not have allowed for the construct of such a Persuasion anyway, and - as was becoming abundantly clear to the First Guardian - not even someone of his Affinity might Weave from the ashes of that which once were!

It should have cut him to the quick, but on this occasion, it did not even irk. Malandar still knew a few 'tricks' and in its stead, he'd done the next-best, simplest thing: nothing but a cheap parlour-trick really; something meant to amuse kids on fest-days and celebrations. It was a folly better suited a 1st Tier Novice, yet the illusion was still worth spinning, for with a little compression of air and a slight bending of light, the horse-coper became as malleable as hot wax. *It was interesting, yet unsurprising. Seemed Harkubsah was indeed a weak fool…*

Malandar blinked, serenely severing the hold.

In response, a shudder seemed to pass through Jab Harkubsah as the illusion vaporised like smoke from an acid burn, and then, as if he had just been pulled from the Void, the man straightened with a gasp as the present came 'rushing back' to envelop him once more.

If he'd been petty, Malandar would have called this experience gratifying. He was not though, and in truth, he felt nothing – not even when the coper gulped down breath after breath, eyeing him with horror now.

"What…?" the man stammered, "Wha… what jus-"

To spare himself the inevitable dribble of words he knew must necessarily come as soon as the horse-monger could muster enough courage to release his tongue, Malandar leaned forward slightly to save the man the trouble.

"No, you were not dreaming!" he offered without mercy, "and yes, I just held you on the cusp of insanity; and yes, you will remember this for a very long time but by your Name: Jab Harkubsah, it is not to be shared."

Swallowing almost painfully slow, the man nodded his obedience but Malandar still carried on, "Now, let this be a lesson to you: be a better person and treat my kind with the respect we are owed! Know that if you or any of your 'associates' come after me - if you conspire to move against me or mine - I will slay every one of you with less ceremony than I would offer rabid Venzoians. Now... consider yourself warned!"

Needing space and not remotely bothered to wait around for any kind of reply, Malandar pushed away from the corral and the ever-unaffected mares, to escape up-wind from the still-speechless man. *He'd done what was needed, and as always, that was all, and-*

Abruptly, something sharp pulled at him, mentally claiming his attention: distracting to the exclusion of all else - and as an invisible hook of recognition continued to bite deeply into his very core, Malandar nearly gasped aloud with a sense of relief.

The Tarvia! Finally...

Finally, the twin reared itself like a true presence in the realm: the hitherto ephemeral sense that had guided this far, suddenly receding before a link that seemed strong and certain like it had done in the past before Marlan shattered the Astral Aide, ripped the flows and left the future wide open to gaping questions. It still tugged at him from out west, though not as far as he might have suspected, or indeed feared.

The First Guardian savoured the pure sensation and allowed himself a smile for the fortune he hadn't been certain of until now. It drew him physically forwards, the familiar pull claiming three full strides out of him before he belatedly recalled time and place and halted mid-step.

Pausing for a moment, but with his heightened senses unfurling like a sail before favourable winds, this new-found link to the Twin left his spirit near woozy from the strength of their re-established connection. Again it compelled him to move, but this time he remained in charge of the purpose and resisted. *It was only right as it should be though! The Tarvia's trail was once more as clear-cut as faceted crystal under the blazing sun: sharp and blinding, rather than murky and masked – and it was his to claim in the name of All!*

Staring like a hungry spirit towards the horizon, Malandar let the heady feeling of 'connection' envelop him completely just a few beats longer. The direction was pure, the arrow of his inner compass pointing near true West, its compelling pressure leaving him ready to pursue. And mercy, it was-

One Call overlaying another; one pattern atop of another…

Surprised, Malandar hissed as the startling sensation rushed through his core. Out of nowhere, the origin of the connection changed subtly – *shifting* - and like a bloodhound scenting just a hint of prey on the breeze, the hunter in him suddenly burned to go claim the Neidar Ba'raie he'd been aware of since crossing over the Boundary.

As though there was a warring in his spirit over which Call to pursue first, both his maze-rune and spirit-rune flared unexpectedly bright along his skin so that for just a single, indeterminate moment it made him want to growl as the presence of 'flawed nature' caught a hold of his interest over that of the Tarvia. *It was not right, but-*

Though his heartbeat never altered, Malandar felt a surge of revulsion roll through his blood, not unlike what he felt when face to face with the Venzoian ilk. It could not be contested that he was staring down a path so different from any he'd ever chosen before as First Guardian of the Upper Circle; so different from anything he'd ever known to practise whilst studying the Deck of Persuasion – and he was about to choose it because reality had left him no other avenue, but it was madness... *there must be something other he could use! And yet...*

Strangely cornered, new impatience welled up. *Itching.* The inherent gift of his ancestry made his blood sing with conflicting ideas but his priorities must remain right; the Tarvia was finally out there, finally, but-

Something fey pulled; for a moment blotting out the light of the Tarvia like an eclipse would the sun. He had horses now; he would be mounted within heartbeats and yet it didn't seem good enough. He could call the Eikyr-

Wrenching back control, the strength of his former convictions instantly weakened sufficiently to become bearable. *Beggars would take and make do with what was given - and without the magic, he felt disturbingly like a beggar, but if he broke the rules he might change that. He might-*

Narrowing his eyes, the First Guardian forced back bloody need with calm determination and the Tarvia's trail strengthened, once more taking up the cardinal position within him. *He still had time to determine his course of action. For now he still just had to travel west, the hard decisions postponed.* He'd be days upon days of hard leagues before catching the Tarvia up and the knowledge acted like a dampener on a chain spell to help him focus far better than the other downright-crazy pull would ever allow.

Black fell, and yet the allure-

He drew a ragged breath. *Time to go!*

Staring directly north-west, as if able to pierce the distance with his eyes, Malandar counted out the agreed payment for the two mares with barely conscious attention to numbers before carelessly dropping the fine plates of pure gold and silver unceremoniously in the dirt at his feet.

"Payment as agreed!" he barked at empty air, gaze riveted one blink longer to the beckoning point beyond the infinite skyline. The contemptuous coper hadn't moved a fraction, but as he turned for the horses, Harkubsah scrambled from his path to retrieve the fee left gleaming in the dirt. *It was like a vulture descending on offal, the riches were picked clean off the ground within moments...*

Malandar favoured the horse-monger a bland stare over one shoulder but the man still flinched, scuttling sideways with half a bow, whilst he clutched the payment to his stomach as though it were entrails about to spill from his severed gut. *The man would not forget the truth of this encounter, but neither could he speak of it. It was possible he'd have hot sweats and sour dreams for a while!*

Snatching up the long reins and the even longer guide rope connected to the grey's bridle, Guardian Malandar Denarlin gripped the saddle, pommel and cantle, mounting the chestnut mare smoothly. *He wasn't entirely convinced by the look of grey's saddle, but still...*

With absent-minded approval, he registered the well-kept sheen of bridles and the worn but carefully oiled saddles and knew himself a little more lucky than expected. Harkubsah had adjusted the stirrup leathers perfectly already, portraying a knowledgeable eye when he wasn't involving himself in crime; a quick check assured him the girth was likewise in order. *Well, wonders and all that...*

"M'lord," the man quavered so softly then, that the First Guardian might not have heard, had he not been who he was, "Wud... wud there b' anything else now?"

Ignoring the question, Malandar turned the horses, preparing to leave. Harkubsah was behind him, yet somehow a tendril of that rancid body-odour crept forth to linger then and his new-found regret was cut mercifully short to be reminded of reality. *Mounted, the stench was just a little less overwhelming, but-*

He halted the chestnut for a beat.

"Well… since you ask,-" he heard himself say, "-for the love of anything dear, you should go take a bath! If in fear of the consequences, I will extend you my personal assurances that out of all the things about to crawl back into this world, this truly will not kill you. You have my sacred promise on that."

Malandar adjusted his seat and almost smiled with genuine mirth, then clicked his tongue at the horse. He didn't need eyes to know Harkubsah's jaw dropped again – this time right in synchronicity with the moment the man went googly-eyed. Perhaps he should have told the coper to go jump off a cliff: the effect might be similar. All in all, of course, it made no difference what the fat man ultimately did, and perhaps with just the smallest hint of lingering contempt burning in his veins, Malandaar'Vahran Denarlin Cor'Esardan turned both horses and his full attention due west.

The mare responded without delay and hopped into a measured trot, the grey following obediently with effortless strides and peaked ears.

He was going to secure the Tarvia and learn of the Alscara's whereabouts, and he would not have much time to see it done – that was where his care lay. Indeed soon, others would be vying to hinder or stop him: the hunter in him sensed it and in this, there was no second place, no prize to be shared – this also figured – and a serene familiarity descended.

Someone had tried to stop him in one sense or another for as long as he could recall, it didn't matter. He would not be denied; he would not forsake the future, nor his vengeance. Not for anything less than the annihilation of his soul and the second death of his body.

And as for the cost…

Well, the cost was the cost; reality was reality. Neither didn't really matter either…

Unease in Friendly Territory

My turn.

Back in his role as escorting officer, Bilan went to Iambre, offering his arm.

This he could do; after months of the same, this procedure was as ingrained as a salute, and in this position, he did not have to wonder at her displeasure with the Master of Banquet's formal words, nor about future or past. It was like a carefully orchestrated parade: all show and pomp, of course, but mercifully he only had to 'endure' a small part of it.

A tick pulled rapidly at his cheek but he ignored it. *Now might very well be the last time he'd ever walk by her side. It made his mind go as numb as his spine – this time with resignation.*

Then Iambre's hand alighted on his arm.

"My thanks to our Knights Commander for his hospitality." Iambre's cool tone was not lost on Bilan, but the official 'prune' never shifted as she sniffed with refined poise: the unmistakable sign of privileged boredom.

The Banquet Master didn't move. Iambre's face barely altered, but her tone held a whip-sharp edge for the need, as she added, "Oh my dear man, you will kink your back! Pray, arise and lead so we may follow as *ordained.*"

Mouth set in a line of professional courtesy, Bilan nudged her with his eyes, perplexed at her behaviour, but she ignored him in favour of the Master of Banquets who finally straightened, though with a small exhale for the strain and a no uncertain quizzical frown of his own.

Iambre did not crack an inch. She'd already slid-on the formal, serene face of the Crown Princess and Bilan saw the 'prune' shake himself

100

almost minutely before he bowed again. *It was old-school dross: Zanzier at its best – or perhaps worst? No one bowed and scraped that much anymore; respect was expected and honoured through action certainly, but never painted on as though in worry the lacquer would crack.*

He expelled rising irritation, for then they were off. Again he was inspired to feel part of a carefully studied dance: one they'd all done countless times; one that he still didn't much care for. Together they joined up behind the stiff-legged Master to follow the old man into the long hallway of desert-coloured sandstone: the pale crystallised silver streaks within the conformation of tight-knit, smoothly hewn blocks clearly proving their provenance the Yellow Snake Province and their age probably somewhere beyond three-hundred summers.

Offering contrast and decoration in the lofty space, numerous freshly-aired runners of pleasant colours and intricate patterns were draped via fabric loops across the continuous black-stained picture rail on either side of the party - the golden silk thread of each design highlighted with a lush gleam under the light afforded by man-sized, ten-pronged silver candelabras that likewise lined the corridor.

To Bilan's nose, the white beeswax added a pleasant smell to that of wood-floor polish - and at four arm-spans-wide, this space fell well within the right margins of 'cosy', so it could surely not be for lack of luxury that Iambre had slanted her lips in a way to signal mild affront.

Ignoring the old lackey half asleep against a bow-legged youth outside the princess' apartments, Bilan nevertheless once more wondered at the spry choice of attendants offered a guest of Iambre's stature, then decided it was none of his concern. Instead, too forgiving of her fickle ways, he resigned himself as he signalled for his men to fall in around their Charge: two slightly in front, two at the rear, the latter just slightly behind Palea, who likewise appeared to be performing her duties with well-oiled perfection. *Everyone knew their places and positions... their duties...*

A stab of satisfaction rushed through him. Sure, the men might not possess the handmaiden's ethereal grace but they possessed the quality that could only come with the seasoning of multiple campaigns. For certain, with or without him, the princess would not lack adequate protection or competent staff, and that was good to know.

He glanced surreptitiously at Iambre from the corner of his eye. Her mien was closed. *Just as well...*

As they walked, the 'prune' began to supply an uninvited stream of running comments and information in regards to places of architectural interest or unusual design, but if the Captain didn't pay it particular mind, he imagined Iambre busy squirrelling away the details, for she was emoting and issuing sounds of interest at what he likewise imagined to be the appropriate moments.

He killed a yawn, the muscles in his face protesting just as Iambre cooed over the ancient fraying carpet, upon which they walked.

The 'prune', of course, lapped up Iambre's attention and soon flourished under this one-woman audience, whilst for lack of better, Bilan found himself instead looking at the halls and galleries, not out of interest but habit.

Castle Zanzier was vast in a way that set him on edge. He'd heard it said on a separate visit that it had been built a thousand years prior to Servangar – allegedly rivalled in age and ugliness only by Ivanor out East. *He could see why.*

He crushed a smile for the contrast between his and Iambre's direction of attention. No doubt, the citadel-like castle had begun as a simple watch-tower long-crumbled to form the legend of the now-thousand-year-old roots but whatever could be said of Zanzier, it was at least well-appointed, and even better than last time too - if one went by the sheer number of Crown Soldiers he'd previously spied both on the walls and in the exercise fields beyond.

Assuredly, he expected little trouble in the middle of the Knights Commander's own abode – however, this was Zanzier: the rat hole of the West. Iambre's safety was paramount and Bilan hadn't survived to the ripe old age of twenty-five autumns by assuming that things couldn't flip upside down in disaster on a moment's notice or in the blink of an arrow's flight from the crossbow. Indeed, experience had taught him a few hard-learned lessons about his supposed superiors and it had resulted in a streak of caution he had no intention of apologising for.

So Zanzier set him on edge…?! Tough chew!

He looked up along the soaring walls of the gallery they were crossing, counting the well-hidden murder holes and ledges running like an unadorned balcony high under the swags of yet more black-stained oak-beams. Doors led from those walkways to Gods-only-knew-where: too many exits in plain view, not enough hidden ones that he could spot – and he didn't like that either.

Gods, there was no particular reason, but the place felt wrong. It was like some unspoken affinity that he could sense it: like one stray alley cat sensing another rival in the vicinity. On his own behalf, the knife in his left boot and the skill of his men would have to suffice, but these days he felt better with a sword by his side as well: a new habit he'd picked up in Etruia and further strengthened by Lieutenant Commander del'Draventar's streak of Esardan paranoia.

Of course, wearing a sword within the inner-keep of an ally during peace-time was damn near considered a hanging offence: only the Lord himself and the soldiers on guard-duty were allowed such arms, but still… *it didn't stop him from wishing he could.*

Glancing sideways at Iambre again, he saw that she'd remained back on form, oozing royalty out of every pore as she walked with the unapologetic grace of a woman who could afford to think of her surroundings in terms of ownership and yearly yield without ever worrying that someone might dare question her right. For now, she was looking nowhere but straight ahead, an engaging mask tied in place with a smile so relaxed it looked real but for the slight strain at the corners of her eyes. It sowed concern. She was still not comfortable, then - yet his was not the place to currently enquire and he submerged himself instead into the sense of 'now', feeling simply her presence, her breath and schooling, as it sieved into his spirit like expensive balm.

Ignoring him now, she looked politely attentive to her surroundings - and so, utterly unapproachable – and as though he needed the flecking reminder: so damned unobtainable!

For mercy the 'prune seemed to have reached a natural gap in his tour of information and it would of course not have been inappropriate for Bilan to make polite conversation to fill the quiet, yet something told him that she needed a little time to forgive him the decision he'd finally forced from her, and so he decided – perhaps wisely for his twenty-five autumns – to remain quiet. *That way, he would not be distracted from using his eyes in the right manner!*

Allowing the slip, he focused for a moment on her hand on his arm. *Her nails gleaned like glass, her signet ring of office and her amber ring of choice set with a halo of diamonds. From their value alone he could feed a street in the Imkarahian slums for a season, maybe more…*

104

He blinked away the discomfort of this contrast too, resuming his former duty of observation, gaze delving into shadowed corners and across arched ceilings. He figured Iambre's given apartments were situated centrally within the keep, some ways from the old banquet hall, which he knew housed within the western quarter; for some reason, the 'prune' seemed to have opted for the scenic tour indeed, taking them down wide carpeted corridors, up the sets of sweeping, shallow stairs, and across two flowing bridges so spindly they gave Bilan the creeps.

For the love of peace of mind, the route was for the most parts deserted – either because everyone had been shooed from their path prior to the old 'prune's' arrival or else because the staff was needed elsewhere with the wealth of guests and visitors currently residing within Zanzier, both town and Keep.

The solitude left him grateful and served to ease his odd mood a little. If memory held true, there'd soon be that last set of broad stairs before the double-width corridor leading on up to the Knights Hall itself - and Gods be good – from the returning strain in his neck and shoulders he hoped he was right. *Then the day would be done… as would he and Iambre.*

For a while then, all he heard was the solid staccato rhythm of his men's stiff uniform boots complimented by the softer click of Iambre's strap-sandals and Palea's whisper of soft slippers.

He should go after this; go catch up on some sword work: grab Kimonar del'Draventar and attempt to thrash him in a ten round duel. Yep, that would help, and-

"Why do you have to be so infuriatingly proper?" Without breaking stride or turning her face towards him, Iambre spoke suddenly and for his ears only.

Bent on thinking little about anything, Bilan swung his face towards her. Engrossed as he'd been in personal reflection, he had to keep the surprise from his face to hear her break the silence.

Fumbling for an eloquent remark, he gave up and simply raised his eyebrows at her: directly in front of them the 'prune' was gesturing, having taken up a lecture on some ancient cut-glass in a south-facing window rosette now. *She ignored the man, though anyone watching would never have guessed.*

"I mean: really? We walk here together, perhaps for the final time, and you give me silence?" Below the whisper, her voice held a slight quiver of accusation though her smile was pleasant as spring flowers.

Bilan cringed. *Well then... beware, you're treading on eggshells here!*

"Highness, forgive me, I guess I was not thinking. "Speaking quietly in turn, Bilan sidestepped the real issue but failed to keep regret from his voice, "Matters have been settled. I assumed you wanted space to think, to place yourself in the right frame of mind so that you might enjoy the evening. I am sure that your presence has been eagerly anticipated."

"Yes! Yes, of course you're right! Bah, you are always so bloody right!" she hissed in an even lower whisper, somehow also adding an encouraging sound of appreciation for something the 'prune' said as she carried on to Bilan, nearly without a breath wasted, "Well thank you, then. I have things on my mind: maddening things and to top it I am now sending you home to Servangar in a little under a dozen days! But sure... a lovely banquet to remind me of all my 'dues' will be just the thing!"

Not knowing what he could possibly respond to that and not anger her further, Bilan kept quiet but she did not appear to notice, and so they walked in renewed silence whilst the 'prune' elaborated on artistically challenging murals until they finally arrived at the mouth of a monumental corridor nearly ten paces wide. From here the tall walls were bare granite, void of décor but for the flanking suits of armour, but little else was needed.

Bilan felt his heart slow a fraction. Before them hovered the massive silver doors of the Knights' Hall – *'an impressive design as any'* the 'prune' had pointed out thus far - and yet Bilan felt no awe as a bereft sense of loss started on collision-course with his heart.

The portal-like entrance shone akin to polished steel, reflecting the torchlight with just a hint of golden sheen to make the bas-relief mouldings of knights on horseback stand out superbly. It was a sight of dramatic luxury. When last here, he'd also heard it told that the old knights of the west had been rumoured to ride their horses to banquet straight upon battle, their ladies awaiting with flowers and wine within.

It seemed a far-fetched fancy though. *For one, where would they put the stinking, sweating, riled up stallions after?*

He smirked minutely, the idea of such an actual melee bemusing, as he pictured horses pooping in the middle of the floor, nudging a lady here to step in said-dump, whilst the Lord's own daughter got slobbered on by the foam-covered mouth of her father's mount seeking out a proffered apple. A thin smile twisted his lips, disappearing like a spirit.

Tonight the corridor smelled only of polished oak and roses. Order ruled and flanking the closed doors stood a quartet of fashionably backwards-attired attendants, in situ only to service the heavy portals as guests arrived and were presented – again in good old Zanzier fashion.

Bilan glanced at the lackeys, his curling disdain for their insipid presence only something imagined, never portrayed. Though no expert, he assumed the lackeys' attire cut in some kind of 'vintage-style throw-back to the Chaos Wars', undoubtedly with the view of impressing the guests with silk, lace and lots of gold trim. The display was peacock-worthy and opulent for Zanzier, he guessed - the hard truth of it much simpler, in that their presence brought his mind right back to the banquet Iambre was about to attend. *She'd be fine. He needed to get over himself; over this edge of unease...*

He coughed, clearing his throat without need. Iambre's small escort was presently the only people in the hallway and all four door-men had perked up markedly at the sight of the princess. *Another ten paces... and then he wouldn't know when he might see her again.*

"Bilandro," she whispered suddenly, so low that he barely heard, "tell me quickly, what is your professional opinion of Castle Zanzier and the town?

Bilan's eye flickered as he almost dropped out of pace. Her face set, calm-beauty still, nevertheless he'd detected an underlying timbre of edge to the princess' question, though surely-

"Tell me: do you feel that we are welcome here?" she questioned urgently, "I mean, truly welcome? Or does it seem to you that the Knights Commander finds our visit burdensome, perhaps even inconvenient?"

The intensity of her words caught and held his attention. Apparently uncaring that they were expected she paused him mid-step, turning now-piercing golden-brown eyes to his.

He hesitated, but she was offering him the deliberately-riveting look he had become accustomed to seeing only when she earnestly sought his professional advice. Not one of the guards seemed to wonder why they did not proceed forward: the princess walked, they walked; the princess paused, they paused. *Easy.* Only the Banquet Master appeared confused as to what action to take, casting discrete glances around the vaulted space, as if answers could be found in the far corners.

Iambre simply ignored the man's fidgeting eyes, expression set in a moue that assured her of a patient frame to await Bilan's response no matter the delay. *And fleck!* It occurred to him that he kept bumping up against the same re-occurring problem... *What to say!*

For what could he say? *Don't trust a soul; this place gives me worse jitters than bedbugs?*

Iambre was not looking for things to worry her further and he would not foist his ill-ideas of uncertainty onto her shoulders. With her present question, she was of course referring to the time of their arrival late last night where their host had seemed less than welcoming – but they'd been days and days late. *Under such circumstance, a semi-disgruntled host might be easily understood.*

He sighed softly. Perhaps Iambre's observation might be the root of these odd vibes he sensed? The woman herself was sensitive to these matters – but perhaps too sensitive now?

He swilled is own unfounded sensations round in his mind as if he could somehow taste their origins, and there was something...

In the short time since their disastrously late arrival here, the general feel of Castle Zanzier had been uncomfortable, he agreed: with servants and staff seemingly... odd.

Furthermore, he might also agree there was something indeterminably surreal about the odd atmosphere that had continuously given him chills ever since his feet had left Raidar's stirrups, but-

But, of course, he could not tell her this outright. It would not help her present mood; distraction was needed...

"I think, that you need not worry Milady: this is the stronghold of the western forces." Bilan kept a formal pose to honour her choice of behaviour, his voice low to stop it from carrying, "Indeed, Milady must rest assured that the retinue is well cared for, as are our men. Only soldiers on active duty are allowed to carry steel within the main keep, but that is only to be seen as good practice. No one has tried to usurp my command, Milady, nor have our weapons been confiscated in the name of 'town peace' or any such madness."

Iambre looked pensive, brow furrowing with a lilting scepticism she savoured for true uncertainty, so he continued, "Highness, since it was night-time upon our arrival, allow me to suggest that perhaps the lack of enthusiasm might have been linked with our own delayed appearance? It did rather… well, it did rather upset the overall state of the entire city I suppose, and I heard it said that the night ran late with ale and less than 'appropriate' Zanzierian behaviour. I guess your appearance incited this celebration and maybe…

"Well, maybe the extra need for armed forces to keep the peace was not appreciated."

Bilan exposed her to a brief smile: a soft version of his best loop-sided expression, cultured to instil light reassurance though dusted with just enough charm to provoke the imagination into meandering in a slightly different direction from whatever current topic in question. "Milady now try to relax? Should you feel unsettled, take heart: these ten days will pass easily, what with all the fine banquets and entertainment in your honour, and then-"

Suddenly aware of his own words Bilan shut his mouth, the reminder of his subtle smile dying on a wince. *Not the best thing he could have chosen to remind her of! Not the best thing at all…*

Solancei's Memoirs

The Province of Tarléon.
Ocean's End.
Autumn of 780 P. C. W.

Tired and weary, I soon let it all blur to abstract, but I'd been right: there was a storm on the way directly from the east, ripping forth on super-frosted winds, gathering low, bringing moisture. It changed the light, lending the scenery a hazy, acidic quality I have now come to associate with magic, but then it was just an eerie, sullen discolouration at our backs. As the sledge flew across the ice, an uneven strip of darkness was beginning to gather across the horizon, and it soon had turned the heavens the colour of blue dirt and ashes. I'd seen it before, but maybe because the State of Veranto had opened my senses, I now also felt the approaching weather like a pressure in my head that warned me just as surely as the skies. *By the night that front would hit Ivanor in a deluge of shard-like needles: dropping temperature and comfort enough to banish even Osari'Chi's Sa'brans back to whence they might originate, and then my parents' graves would be lost; swallowed by the new ice, and the old.*

I felt strangely lethargic though. My fear for Rainan had stripped away and I found it didn't matter; knew he would be back well in time before the weather hit, though I could not have explained how I knew.

See, I honestly don't know if the Veranto was still bleeding into me or if I'd simply spend myself through natural measures, but something in me went lax: I was packed within layers of costly pelts; warm and snug at last. *'Long-haired polar fox and snow hares',* I recalled once hearing Taliana exclaim with a most satisfied lilt to her voice upon seeing the costly Kheltian gift. *'How wonderful…''*

Yes… wonderful… yes…

And that's exactly when a strange thing happened. *I 'heard' the word 'wonderful' echoing in my head, and then-*

111

Something I always since thought of as 'an icicle the length of an arm' speared through me: directly down through the very crown of my head; slash!

It didn't hurt, but I felt hurt as it cleaved me in half.

Suddenly so hot I could barely breathe, I exhaled one hard breath. I remember the terrible feel of it: as though it might be my last - and then, just as abruptly, I no longer sped over the snow-dusted ice-sheet in a stately sledge, but found myself instead unexpectedly transported to the confines of my parents' insulated, stuffy coach.

It was odd; not a single blink passed, then-

I felt strange: a shadow of myself if you like – the transition too swift for me to align with the present, and yet it held a flavour of reality as I gawked at the four faces turned my way as though my sudden appearance had not ruffled nor surprised. *The eyes of dead people very much alive stared at me as if I had presumed to interrupt an adult conversation with a titbit of unimportant nonsense: I knew the look well...*

On top of everything, it was more than I could cope with. In the next blink my emotions welled high and my eyes filled with the tears I hadn't permitted myself earlier when I'd attempted to honour Taliana and had somehow embraced the State of Veranto.

Yet these tears were of relief. *Relief and joy! It was all going to be fine; everything was all alright after all! A bad dream; I'd just had a really bad dream!*

As though to mock my perception, everything became fuzzy and safe – almost overwhelming me with new contentment. *All right. It was going to be all-*

The carriage keeled alarmingly as it hit a deep pothole, rocking everyone, but with a sort of wooden mechanics that felt unreal in view of such a hard jolt - and my sense of relief rolled away down my back like a fat drop of cold sweat then. In less than a blink, a fey strangeness filled me like a crushing spring-time wave topped with slush and debris, and it seemed my life got overtaken by all kinds of weird, then.

'Weird' is never good. I have learned this recently, and magic has a lot to do with that, however in a manner of speaking I suppose I would have embraced

'weird' like an old friend if I'd known what came next! Because then 'gruesome' took over and 'weird' no longer mattered, as I was somehow forced to witness my parents, and Taliana, and several household staff, all die in a way that would have made most grown men fall to their knees and praise every fickle God beyond the Veils that they would spare them from similar fate!

So did my loved ones perish in an accident or did the whispers do justice to the hidden truth?

Well, there are accidents… And then there are… *Accidents;* I challenge you to guess which way this one sways! Take whatever horror you can imagine, then triple it, and wipe a smile off its face for the cruel trick it should never have played on you, and maybe you'll come close. Maybe…

Oh and also, did I mention that the State of Veranto brings clarity? Hmm… well… yes… would that its supernatural gifts had brought me the answers that I craved too, but maybe that would have been cheating?

Solancei

Unexpected Bargain

Iambre offered him a weak, thankful smile regardless of the inappropriate reference - a warmth of sadness and understanding there in her eyes for only him to see. Then she shrugged. "I feel... I feel different here, Bilan. There is something...

"Well, I cannot tell you, but something has happened and it has made me feel like... like something awful is about to come down on all of us. Am I just... just too touchy perhaps?"

Her awkward attempt at describing the feeling permeating this place, made him smile again: genuine affection now. *Had something happened? What?* He wanted to ask but it was not appropriate. He wanted to hug her and tell her that she was fabricating; instead, he lightly stroked his thumb along the curve of her right hand where no one could see.

"Milady, there is a lot to be said for the reputation of the Crown Princess' personal guard,-" he remarked, a light quiver raising his brow, "-and there is even more to be said for the honour and reputation of the Knights Commander of the West. Remember that he is a busy man and that he does not usually need to conform to the needs of royal guests. He may simply feel frustrated by the idea of a week cooped up in his castle, when really he should be out overseeing training and drilling our forces. If you look there - you might find the root of his reluctance."

Iambre nodded slowly and he carried on, certain dismissal of suggested mysteries colouring his voice, "Everyone knows that under the cover of shadows and night, all appears much worse than what daylight may reveal. You have only been here one day. Give the place a chance, Milady. I have sensed no problems to concern us. The guards of the Keep are competent and professional, and I dare say that we should suffer no incidents here."

Bilan held her eye, his outer calm never in jeopardy, and yet…

And yet… stranger things have been known to happen within supposedly friendly territory – be wary my love!

Iambre looked around, seemingly calm too - but resting her eyes briefly on Palea's patient form, Bilan knew that the princess was making sure that they still could not be overheard.

Palea glanced at her Lady in soft query: big innocent eyes widening for a moment as she imagined herself needed, but Iambre bestowed a reassuring beatific smile upon her handmaiden, then turned the two of them away. Though still holding Bilan's arm very lightly, she managed to send the Master an apologetic nod also.

"Your persuasions echo those of Chief Eso," she allowed in a soft whisper, "For a wonder, it was only just last night that she said near-to-the-word the same things to me. And you are both right, of course. And Gods… I feel so rather silly to admit I've been spooked without cause but whatever is said or done between us, I value your opinion and felt a need to speak."

Frown playing hopscotch across her forehead, her voice dropped a notch though it hardly seemed possible, "Did you realise that the Knights Commander good as ordered me to attend his gathering tonight? As you heard: his choice of words was… was inelegant, and-

"Well, I wonder how he could imagine I would not notice and take offence?"

Semi-relieved by the direction of her words, for a blink he almost didn't take her complaint seriously and Iambre's eyes crinkled with stealthy nuisance as she looked at Bilan. "Of all the people in the realm, *he* sees

through fingers with something so fundamentally ingrained in protocol? Why?

"Why, when everything else is so… so infuriatingly old-fashioned! What is he thinking? There is no need for him to be so crass - but he is, of course, the only person powerful enough to get away with such a slight, and perhaps he is just being obnoxious because he can, but it's-"

Iambre paused for breath, her fingers twitching as though in need to ball her hands like a child, but she controlled it and instead her voice picked up in a confounded hiss, "Gods Bilan, by all good rights… in response to such oversight, I should be in my apartments still: refusing his company. But then… but then I would have missed this time with you!"

"Milady, you flatter me…" Bilan shifted his weight from one foot then back again, mind fusing into a basket of knotted-up yarn upon recalling her earlier behaviour in response to the Banquet Master. *Flattered… yes… but he had to stop feeling like that.*

"Look, I do not pretend to know what drove the Knights Commander to display such poor protocol, but perhaps he got it wrong?" *No, he wouldn't have…*

Flicking his head almost imperceptibly towards the impatient Master of Banquets, Bilan let a note of reason creep into his lowered voice, "Perhaps it's the 'prune's' fault? Like I said, the Knights Commander is perhaps just not appreciative of the fact that his castle has been turned on its head – even if it is for the Crown Princess herself. And why would Zulavi wish to cause slight? He is generally well-respected by everyone, Milady."

Bilan let the assurance filter into his eyes as he struggled to soften the hard cast settling into his jaw. *There was little reason, but somehow he detested the western bastard. No need to let her be privy to that little fact though.*

"Yes… yes, I am sure you are right." Iambre sighed, too much air escaping in one breath: she was capitulating.

As though inspired, the Master of banquet mirrored her… not capitulating… concerned!

Etruian-taught tolerance holding no bearing, Bilan shifted his gaze from the 'prune' with small care for the offence he knew a scowl would inspire. Voice lowered to little louder than a soft sigh, he said, "Milady, I can take steps to ensure that you feel a little more armoured to deal with the Commander should the need arise? If it would prevent you from worrying, should you wish it, I can order the men to observe *Right of Command.* If done, whatever Zulavi might say, he will speak to no avail for they will not relinquish you from sight. It is… it is usually reserved for slightly more fractious circumstances, but if you wish it-"

"I wish it," she injected.

"He might take slight," Bilan warned her with a slanting smile.

In return, Iambre flashed him a hard wolfish smile. "Oh well, tit for tat. In the interest of diplomacy, I will try my hardest to let go of my dislikes, and I shall certainly take satisfaction in the fact that I have now made him wait. Tit for tat, indeed!"

Clever woman! Iambre was wise enough to know that diplomacy must prevail and she'd never stir something at the banquet that she would later regret. Bilan almost kissed her again - keeping a cool head was not the easiest thing – but he yanked back on the urge as though it was physical. *The cast to her eyes held edgy concern. Something had her ruffled indeed, and besides… this was over! Even were they not in public with nearly a dozen witnesses, it was over! So what to say…*

"Milady, the Knights Commander is a military leader, trusted by many, including your own good parents and half the Senate. A few skivvy

Zanzierian comments will be easy for you to ignore. I know you will do well."

"You are correct - and yes, I will listen to your counsel, have no fears on that account. Now, regretfully I must bid you good night before the Master begins to chew on his own staff in frustration-" Iambre's beautifully painted mouth sliced into a grin of wicked quality, "-and alas, I really I don't think I could bear that on my conscience."

Despite misgivings, Bilan laughed under his breath with genuine mirth at the mental picture wrought by her words and Iambre's own grin widened for a beat, then faded before new seriousness.

"I meant what I said Bilan," she told him in sombre honesty, "I love you. You should know that I will try to find a way to call on you before we part."

His heart jumped, the rest of him twitched painfully, but she'd already let go of his arm, turning from him and motioning for Palea to come join her before he had the chance to utter a response. The Master of Banquet looked relieved; Bilan was not. His task was completed and he brought the guards to attention with all but one look, all of them saluting the princess smartly as she turned one final time to incline her head in thanks and dismissal. Then the impressive doors opened and light blazed forth along with heat, music, and a general, indistinct buzz of many voices mixing.

As had been the case on other occasions, Bilan was offered a brief view of a closely packed hall beyond: it was a melting pot of people, gold, silk and smells; the ceiling was hung with heraldry; what was visible of the walls revealed antique weapons best left in history books, but displayed to excess in wide rosettes, one size and style organised within the other, forming circles flanked by sweeping fans.

Unsurprising, the music cut off mid-note and a hush descended then, dampening the voices in line with the Banquet Master's appearance. For a few heartbeats anticipation made the air seem charged with something akin to the buzz that lingered after a lightning strike; then the Banquet Master ruined the effect, stomping the staff into the floor for attention, before droning, "All welcome, all hail the Crown Princess Iambre…"

The remainder of the announcement becoming an indistinct blur of sounds in his ears, for a moment Bilan hated his own existence. It was the same wherever they visited: protocol made few allowances for alterations. Iambre tilted her head a fraction and prepared with a deep breath that revealed a sifter of her sometimes fractious disposition, then she exhaled it like a man about to step on the scaffold, and disappearedthrough the fifteen-foot portal as though already Queen.

He pulled his eyes back where they belonged a little too late as usual. Lights off the numerous dropped-down chandeliers set off the pale gold of her hair and the lustre of her dress, with enough metallic sparkle to entice a dragon to come steal more treasure, and again something seemed to tear at his innards. *When these ten days were up, it'd be damnable hard to mount his horse and turn back north-east, but he'd do it rather than risk her reputation - they'd danced around that fire for too long – but if he should be pleased that she'd finally relented, how come then he felt so flecking dejected?*

The team of retainers slowly drew close the double doors, drawing Bilan's mood further into black. He did not like this place: the corridor seemed suddenly shrouded in a deeper, more sombre light than earlier, and with Iambre so oddly uneasy about Knights Commander Zulavi, he wished he could walk with her, if only to tell the Commander – noble or not – to back the fleck off and show some respect!

Anger swilled, but unwilling to allow himself the pleasure, Bilan focused on his work instead: barking necessary orders at the four guards.

Ironically he wasn't required to wait with the men; Iambre was supposed to select a guest of her choice to perform the honour of escorting her back to the chambers, but she also needn't pick one, for the Master of Banquet would be at hand to lead the way regardless. Of course, her guards remained on duty for the duration, simply for show. He could stay but that would look strange! *It left Sergeant Seiman - a greying whippet of a man - the one in charge now. The weather-beaten veteran had never failed him, but...*

"You know the drill," he told Seiman regardless, with a nod for the closed doors, "but when the Lady comes to leave later, tonight you will invoke the *Right of Command* in my name and you will not allow anyone to gainsay this unless Her Grace gives you leeway."

Sergeant Seiman grunted. "If those are your orders, then we will oblige. Do you fear trouble, Captain?"

Bilan hesitated, then declared, "Perhaps Sergeant, but not of the usual kind. Her Ladyship will simply feel better knowing that you cannot be dismissed by some higher ranking lackey without my permission."

At that Seiman grunted again and with one final salute, Bilan wretched his thoughts back to elementary things, sadly never caring to note whether his men would return the honour as prescribed as they slackened their stances and halberds to hunker down for the wait. Iambre's unease seemed to reverberate within his core still, but he was powerless to alleviate it; in truth, Knights Commander Zulavi - one of the highest-ranking field generals of the realm - had never set a foot wrong and he was furthermore considered one of the best strategic assets the provinces had ever known. *Why did he not feel right?*

Striding out down the wide corridor, Bilan clasped his belt and allowed thoughts to drift.

The time Iambre's retinue spent here would fly – particularly now that he knew he'd be leaving at the end; he could not afford to linger on an unsubstantiated idea about a man who had nothing but honour and true service to his name, whilst also expecting to perform an adequate handover to his circle of commanding officers. It'd be hard enough to keep his wits honed when the knowledge of leaving Iambre would linger at the forefront of his mind until the very moment she put the documents of goodbye in his hand, effectively dismissing his services once and for all, and-

For a tormenting moment, the memory of their heated embrace rose up to haunt, and with it a kernel of renewed desire sparkled in the pit of his stomach, but it wouldn't do!

Dragging his mind from the image of him and Iambre together, he deliberately pictured her handmaidens instead.

Why had the Gods not been kind enough to make one of them the centre of his attraction instead? Sure as thunder before lightning, that would have been so much easier to deal with, not to say acceptable!

Blood and guts! It was not talked about, but he had of course seen them all without their veils and even if the Viper might best be described as 'interesting', the other two were easy on the eye! *Ah but if only…*

Bilan reached an intersection and paused. *Shouldn't he have reached the right adjoining corridor by now?*

Slightly annoyed but suddenly not certain if he'd gone too far or not far enough, Bilan looked up to see a thoroughly ugly tapestry of two black monsters devouring a twin-horned creature that might be said to harbour a certain semblance to a horse. A fabled creature, its name escaped him, yet the image made him curse to the fleck out loud. *He was nearly at the end of the corridor: the unsavoury wall hanging heralding a natural T-junction, and he had no idea where either route might take him!*

Cussing the Gods under his breath, Bilan spun around. He should have had the wherewithal to ask the retainers to clarify the best way for him to reach the mass hall. From there he'd recall the way back to the men's quarters, but his head had been elsewhere, hadn't it!

With a vexed sigh, Bilan Metavo – Royal Marshall, Commanding Officer and Captain of the King's Legion, started backtracking his steps.

This here was not what he had bargained for when he'd joined the forces! Not what he'd bargained for at all! Curse his fate, but when it came to Iambre he just couldn't seem to think straight: somehow she slurred his senses till he was little more than a mindless fool and it was high time it got put to an end, except...

Well, except even as he acknowledged the truth of this, even as he knew that Iambre had finally chosen the right path for the both of them, there was ever a cursed treacherous part of him that screamed he must somehow make her change her mind back again. That he must!

Inspired to feel the need of a drink, he swallowed, mentally stabbing the lingering emotion dead and stamping down hard on the voice of trouble.

No, this was not what he'd bargained for at all. Not. At. Bloody. All.

Back on the Road

Where the fleck am I?

Startled awake from the depths of dreamless stupor by an inexplicable perception of danger, Solancei registered only three things: one, the pungent stench of urine; two, that her wrists had been tied together in front of her chest; and three, that she was on the ground!

Deep-seeded reflexes had her moving before she was fully awake to perceive the mistake it would be to do so, and the backlash of her rash action was near-instant. Total disorientation gripped her, an impenetrable darkness smothered, yet urgent alarm died within a fateful heartbeat when the jolting move made the aggravation of multiple injuries cut through her resolve like a scythe obliterating life.

Body convulsing, mind turning blank, a scream rend the silence as she collapsed back onto elbows and knees, the unforgiving surface lending little relevance to her existence as the sounds of her own agonised intakes of air bisected on hard sobs of pain wrung forth on each new breath.

As though she'd run beyond her endurance, she was hopelessly winded; couldn't move; paroxysms played her body like a broken instrument, raising a tingling notion of panic that only doubled because it somehow couldn't quite sear through the haze.

Why should she hurt like this? She had no recollection and the 'lack' pierced her with a spear of frenzy; again she tried to move, but injury kept her down whilst the world tilted inside her head to promote another lance of pain.

She gasped, feeling thin stale air whistle through her open mouth, yet achieving no quarter. The effort of staying on the wakeful side of oblivion seemed too monumental for pursuit; whatever was wrong with her 'waited' for another two breaths, then pounced...

She felt something spiralling... realised it was her... but then the darkness within was rising.

Out of habit, she reached for the State of Veranto to lend succour, failed, and for a moment stars danced like fireflies in her mind, while she reeled like a steep tower staircase, going round and round on itself to compliment a staccato headache that matched the rhythm of her heart with one beat's delay. Then the blisters of light receded and her skewed body managed to reform into a mode of self-preservation where it finally caught up with a semblance of its former ability to function. She managed a weak breath then. *So careful, it seemed she was straining, but it held the ache at bay; mercy...*

Her faculties restored, so did the awareness of the dark and the smell of urine return, and it occurred to her that she was damp everywhere. Vaguely, she wondered if she'd peed herself or if the stench came from somewhere else, but a fleeting concern, the question of whether she'd fouled herself or not seemed unimportant in comparison with her overall predicament.

She shivered, remembering a beat too late that she should have controlled it, but when the small action pushed her over the edge of comfort to bring back the lance of internal fire, the idea lost cohesion. Gasping shallow breaths, she sued for control, and mercifully regained a little.

Why was she injured? What had happened? The soup in her head was smothering...

Wild thoughts jumbled up, she struggled to stay focused, to remain conscious, but her persistence only seemed to make matters worse and she gagged, assaulted by a sudden urge to empty her insides.

She managed nothing but bile, then the heaving floored her anew. *The pain wanted her; she couldn't fight it: her body gave out, then her mind. Then… nothing.*

When she came to again, Solancei simply lay there, feeling battered but not in outright agony providing she did not move or breathe too deeply. She was drained. This time she had no room for panic and the pungent stench of urine seemed less pronounced than earlier. There was a harsh, foul taste in her mouth – *metallic* - but though she tried to swallow repeatedly, her throat was too dry to humour saliva.

She sniffed - the tip of her nose icy, bordering on numb. It seemed the only thing in her body that was detached beyond hurt. *Well, discounting her tied hands…*

She sniffed again. Not sure of the passing of time; not sure how long she'd been unconscious, but she was nevertheless better able to take stock of herself now, pathetic comfort it may be. A shortness of breath prevailed, as did a building need for answers, but it didn't seem to follow that her mind was going to oblige. Her head throbbed; her entire body seemed a bonfire of aches and pains that assured her she must have been 'painted' blue and green by something. *But how? And when?*

Solancei blinked as though it might clear her mind. *She didn't quite seem able to recall anything recent.* Her thoughts came too slow and with reluctance – like she was asking a senile valet in residence to dredge up old dreams he'd somehow misplaced.

Pitch surrounded her. *Perhaps she should be thankful – but then again, maybe not?* It was thick like a horse blanket, covering her senses - yet the more aware: the more the air seemed to cool her skin till she feared she'd been shoved down Arbar'Chi's maw: a place without compromise or ending. *And Gods, from there-*

Oh from there it took precious little imagination to believe that the God of Death had in fact already thrown his hood over her eyes, so that accustomed to the darkness of forever, she could be carried off Beyond!

She shivered, instantly regretting, as the pain sliced through her. It dissipated, and she tried to lie still, then.

Her thoughts were sluggishly churning. *Why was she here?* Her mind remained as dark as night too, somehow incapable of recalling.

And where was the light? Her eyes were wide open but she had no way of judging her surroundings. *Was she dead? Something about Arbar'Chi's hood haunted her, or was that something else?*

Confusion stuck, then lifted as her thoughts filtered apart. The air still seemed old and lifeless; she could taste her loneliness within the dank mouldy reek that spelt 'ancient' and 'subterranean' in the same breath. *But why?*

Loath to add further to her hurts Solancei pushed a number of imaged scenarios from her mind. A distant, lazy drip-drip-drip of water registered as the only sound in this otherwise deadened darkness and her mind twisted, the effort in vain as the uncomfortable void did not budge.

She thought she'd hit her head, had she not? But how? And why had she woken up in a black hole with her hands bound and without a single person to see to her? Uncomfortable, clammy and cold, the twine around her wrists made her feel like a criminal and though it might cost, she tried to shift to relieve a sudden acute fear of the unknown as it drilled deeper into her core. *She was not a criminal. What was wrong with her memory? Why could she not recall?*

Her questions received no answer, curse Osari'Chi - for with his usual predictability, the puzzling God of Confusion hid away all answers behind a casual lack of response and she was too tired to focus for long.

Breathing carefully, she tried instead to shift herself into a less compromising position, but a butterfly of pain fluttered its wings lightly down her left side. It sparked certain details back into light: *a cold evening, detours and delays along the Zanzier roads, Iambre complaining...* but none of that seemed appropriate to explain her present state, nor the situation, and on the back of more uncertainty, that singular wave of panic rose once more, threatening to choke her. *She didn't want to pass out again! Gods be kind – she did not!*

Solancei swallowed painfully, her mind slewing to a halt.

She was usually made of a sturdier, more level-headed spirit than this and it was so disturbingly unlike her to be undone by a little trouble that she did manage to wrench a measure of self-control back before further hysterics marched in to fill the gaping holes in her mind. *Well... at least she remembered her name... and Iambre... and the Chief... at least...*

New feelings stirred then, and in a flash her mind flew to Chief Eso Mehadja and this woman's many schemes and machinations in the name of 'Crown Protection'. *Yes, she most certainly remembered the Chief as well! Could this be one of Klaas' elaborate trials?*

Part of her would have liked to think it so, whilst another, more realistic part seemed disinclined to agree. The situation carried a stink of 'wrongness' about it, which easily assured her that even with her mind temporarily clogged up, this could not just simply be about 'training'. *Oh sure, Chief Eso could be devious, but this... this felt different!*

Giving her mental block one last futile kick, her mind spun from the unknown to recent events that she *did* remember: her problems with the State of Veranto... Iambre and Captain Metavo... the seemingly never-ending route to Zanzier... and it struck her then that perhaps something had happened to her on the road?

Perhaps she had taken another fall from South-Point and this time cracked her head open?

It seemed possible, though not plausible. For one, she was wearing leathers; semi-damp, cold leathers that were starting to chafe and add additional discomfort to her current state of misery, but leathers just the same, which - comfort aside - did not fit. On the road, she was 'just' Iambre's chief handmaiden. Which meant that on the road, she'd never wear this sort of outfit; the leathers were for training. What was she missing? *Perhaps something about a jackal fight?*

Other ideas swelled and dissolved, none of them sticking in her mind, and confusion rocked her anew. *She was so tired; too tired to puzzle this out. She just wanted a warm bed...*

Solancei shifted her bound fists slightly left to alleviate an uncomfortable onset of pins and needles up her arms and paid for the adjustment as someone 'buried' a dull hatchet in her lower ribcage.

Pulling a face in the darkness, it made her pose on an exhale, stuck but slowly able to adapt. She'd been injured before; she knew her own body intimately; knew what broken bones felt like, and with every breathless puff she only half-managed to suck into her lungs, there was an equal straining in her side that left her little doubt that she'd cracked several ribs. *But Gods...? How? How? How?! And where was the Medic?*

She closed her eyes - or perhaps they were already shut? – but regardless of what they were, her thoughts seemed to disintegrate then - as though her capacity to hang on to anything of import simply withered under the onset of fatigue.

It was a relief. She let it happen. *And she dreamed, then.*

Or, at least it felt like a dream, but at the same time it also seemed a strangely lucid experience - as though she was on the constant cusp of

128

awakening – and she could not really be certain. *Perhaps,* she mused, *she was in fact not dreaming at all, but wide awake rather and right where she was supposed to be: in the familiar surroundings that she knew so well?*

For a moment, she felt split and uncertain, but here there was no pain, no aching body to contend with and without any trouble at all, dream became reality - *or perhaps*, she conceded, *it was just reality that became dream?*

She let the concept drift, feeling something familiar, yet unable to name it. A strange shift in perception made her mind waver as she struggled to pinpoint her own location and then she found herself suddenly back on the Zanzier road, long skirts swishing around her calves as she marched from Iambre's presence with ire in her heart and a fire in her gaze.

They were feelings that anchored. The scene was so familiar, she thought; just as she recalled it, a small voice commented from the back of her mind. *The last rays of a beautiful sunset seemed unusually determined to brighten the skies for just a few moments longer this evening, and it was a stupendous display of fiery colours: a sight that she might even have stopped to gaze upon if this had been a normal evening. But Gods, today it wasn't! Today, she just wanted the day gone! Gone; gone; gone!*

The fine weeds and gravelled dirt beneath her boots crunched softly with every long stride that it reminded her for a moment of how thirsty she still was from a long day of breathing road-dust, but she stubbornly refused to give in to it. *Giving in would mean going back!* Oh and the mere idea of capitulating made her anger simmer yet a couple of degrees hotter as her busy strides ate away the ground in stark contrast with the picture she was otherwise presenting to the world. *A picture, of a lady of standing, with kohl-rimmed eyes, silver ribbons with tiny leaves draping off her hair and cuff-bracelets to match; a lady dressed in fitted embroidered-cotton of the ankle-*

length variety, which definitely warranted 'gliding', not marching; a lady who should've been wearing her veil, yet suspiciously gloried in the partly-undone spirals of hair that currently bounced with delicious freedom across her shoulders for every brute stride.

She clenched her teeth. *Now see if she cared what image she presented?! If only she'd been an Ice Dragon, she would have frosted them all – with particular attention to Iambre, first and foremost! Particular attention...!*

An upended cup of a dice and circles reflected loudly in the background, interrupting her thoughts, as some feller spat a good-natured curse at his bad luck only to nod in contrite apology when she glared his way. *Bad luck indeed – was there any other kind? The air reeked of tangy wood smoke, celeriac soup, toasted herbal bread and salted bacon; there were camp fires everywhere, the tranquil streamers rising high to weave the illusion of a canopy over the temporary settlement and she'd flecking well march if she wanted to - even if Cook's apple pie smelled divine and might have swayed her!*

And there it was. At that moment, a sense of déjà-vu struck her. As if all of this had already happened days and days ago, but she shook it off. Her mind was playing too many tricks on her these days. She would have recalled this scenery: the gnarled, but proud trees, the sandy, tight-packed road with the cracked illegible stone markers, the odd detrimental heinar in full flower, the jolting pace of people frustrated-past-care of a slip of the tongue, the black gnats descending at night, the flinty outcrops rising tall like the petrified fins of old dragons framing their journey. *As it happened, the monotony alone made it all too memorable!*

Walking on, she pushed the notion firmly aside and finally reached past the last circle of fires to pass the sentries on guard with little more than a glance. They knew her of course, and let her through without a word, but the odd sense of displacement was slow to disperse. For some strange reason, she had a nagging sensation that there was something out of place; something not quite right. As she continued to walk, it felt as though she was following a path from which she was incapable of deviating: there seemed a certainty about her steps and pace that made her think she could almost recall what was about to happen next, but that was silly too. *Her temper was as real as the leisurely un-bound hair on her head, and all the while her displeasure continued to blaze - she was annoyed with Iambre,-*

No, she corrected herself: *not 'annoyed', flecking livid, actually! And her anger was real! Real enough to scorch, for this time her friend had gone too far!*

Gods, but it hadn't seemed possible it would ever come to this, but Iambre was now stooping so low as to feign tantrums over their delays, which she by default of her own actions had created for herself – and it was ludicrous beyond fault, when really it was but a smoke-screen to cover for the real object of her frustration: Captain Bilandro Metavo!

Now normally, Solancei would have forgiven the Princess, but her friend's 'indulgence' was happening a little too often for comfort these days and she'd just about had enough! She shook her head with a curt unrealised gesture that set the silver in her hair tingling like a set of tiny chimes.

'No, not this time!', she repeated to herself.

Her wretched friend was fuelling a fire about Captain Metavo's consistent lack of 'co-operation' in regards to certain sensitive matters that were better left unspoken – *'apparently'* - and it was becoming more and more a problem.

Only *she* knew of the real reason behind their tempestuous princess' thunderous mood swings, but Solancei was currently just as fed up as anyone else, except *she* wouldn't stoop to 'commenting' on the fact behind the Princess' back. *And flecking comment they did,* Solancei thought with a frown. Comment on the rise in Her Ladyship's 'spoiled tendencies' and 'ill-considered ideas'.

This is so unlike her' they'd say, and Solancei had seen how Iambre's image had taken a dive as she was rapidly going from being 'adored' by her staff, to being 'abhorred'. *And all just because of a stupid crush! All just because...*

Gods, but for the love she held for her friend, Solancei had kept the secret and acted her part, which - to take the brunt interest off Iambre - had often ended with staff cursing *her foulness* rather than the princess', but it couldn't be helped; people had sort of grown to expect such things from the Heiress' cousin, so that was fine, really. But even if she'd played along; and even if she'd carried her share of the problem; enough was enough! Iambre was behaving like a disgraceful brat, and if Solancei couldn't very well let on the truth to anyone without repercussions, then neither could she stand much more of Iambre's brazen abuse of their lifelong friendship. *Bilandro-flecking-Metavo! Would that they'd never laid eye on him! Would that he'd stayed in Imkarah's notorious Lake Side, where rumours and boasts would often have him placed prior to Etruia!*

Solancei huffed out a breath of pent-up air to alleviate her own smouldering wrath and stalked left. The Heiress' behemoth of a camp was within a good stone's throw still but she knew better than to veer off in the deepening twilight, only to twist an ankle or worse in one of the many tricky alterations this terrain seemed to hold tight to until the very moment of disaster. *Bilan! Always ruddy Bilan!*

Another huff escaped her, yet cursedly she knew just a tinge of guilt to mentally slight the man who'd done nothing worse than catch the Crown

Princess' interest with his stupidly heroic stunts and the glory of a mission deemed impossible. *How did Iambre imagine this would end?* The man was low-born - nothing but a near-peasant, though he'd scrubbed up well - and still so far beneath the Princess' station that he was never even meant to have met her in the first place.

Well, crap and guts! Courtesy of deeds and curiosity, the man had defied the laws of society and done just that regardless. One had to admire the pluck, of course, yet from the very first moment, Solancei had seen Iambre look into the flecking man's dark, deep eyes, things had gotten complicated! Iambre was moon-struck; didn't appear about to get herself 'un-stuck' any time soon, and Solancei was fed up with the pretence that everything was fine; fed up with her friend's selfish needs; fed up being in the middle; fed up acting the 'witch'; fed up being treated as one!

She kicked angrily at a large pebble and watched it fly from her unchartered path in a shallow arch whilst her mind rolled back one more time to the painful event she now stalked to outpace.

Again, she saw the three of them standing amidst the plump Tuxaman cushions and low Iddian tables of the Princess' hastily erected pavilion, the argument that would prove to inspire conflict rapidly developing. *And again,* her blood seemed to stream molten through her veins with the thought of Iambre's uncouth behaviour. *The Princess ought to know better, but evidently not.*

"How can a wheel that was serviced less than a week ago, so suddenly break?" Iambre flung the words like a personal accusation as she rounded on Captain Metavo in exasperation upon hearing the news of yet another delay. "Are you personally making up these things just to vex me, Captain?! Or, are you lot simply incapable of getting this train to move from A. to B. without mishaps?!"

For a blink the Captain bristled at her choice tone, but it came as no surprise when he managed to keep his cool. As expected, he simply refrained from trying to reason with the Princess and like so many times before, Solancei watched him draw one of those careful breaths that seemed to serve him so well, though this time, it did not quite cover for the hint of disbelief that briefly flickered across the planes of his olive, tanned face. *Oh, the fool...*

"Well, the roads are winding..." Solancei stepped in and made the would-be helpful comment in a non-committed manner, partly to spare the Princess words she'd most certainly regret, and partly to help the Captain, who - in spite all else – did not truly deserve her friend's unreserved ire over these kinds of banalities.

"What?" Iambre turned her malignant gaze from Bilan to spare her an arched look that could have belonged on a hunting hawk disturbed from catching its prey by a rustle of wind in the bushes, "The roads are 'winding'? My, are you our 'official navigator' now, or was that simply just another comment to test my patience to the fullest?"

Eyeing them both angrily, Iambre looked ugly as her golden brows drew down and her spine lengthened to draw her up tall. "Honestly people... do you really think me that cloud-brained? Gods defend me: you act like a pair of village idiots!"

"Milady, please, you misunderstand." His slurred Imkarahian accent becoming momentarily pronounced, Bilandro Metavo interjected the denial a little too fervently, his dark eyes widening with criminal honesty as he spoke to pacify Iambre. *And dear Gods, looking like that, even Solancei might forgive the Captain a thousand slights, but Iambre only quivered dismissively, the action setting the delicate layers of her pearl robe floating as though a bird ruffling its feathers.*

Solancei exhaled hard and flashed her friend a narrow-eyed look, questing, "Verily? Village idiots?"

Iambre snorted, her thick, casual plait almost bristling with something akin to independent life, as she rolled her eyes dismissively. "Lancei come on! Both of you appear to be idiots!"

Solancei felt her face twitch as though Iambre had just cut open a rotten orange spilling a sweet-and-sour stench with a handful of maggots. *Unsurprisingly, new levels of disdain made her want to slap the Princess. Unsurprisingly, she didn't.*

"Please watch just whom you're calling an idiot now," she growled instead, voice tight, low-pitched – *not so much interested in pacifying!*

Unlike Bilan, she was not a fool who needed approval, and besides, Iambre could never make her cower – a thing the Heiress well-knew!

In return, Iambre snorted with mocking amusement. Alternating her eyes from her to Bilan and back again. *Had venomous intent been airborne, her cousin the princess-impossible would've slain them both with her amber gaze.*

In turn, Solancei tilted her chin, riling her friend with a frosty smile, then cocking an eyebrow, silently daring the princess to make another comment: silently daring her to say just the 'right' wrong thing.

It was odd because at the same time she wanted to laugh at the idiocy. Oh, but how love was a tangled thing! A useless, tangled thing, indeed! Iambre looked like a small thundercloud. Pretty, but ominous…

Something of her feelings must have shown on Solancei's face after all then, for Iambre's glare intensified. *Here we go…*

"Lancei," Iambre barked in a voice laced with indignation, "if you do not take kindly to my words, then stop for a moment and listen to yourself! Gods, if either of you object to my comparisons then don't act the part that places the connotation in my mind to begin with. Surely that is not too hard. You are both clever people!"

Iambre threw the last words specifically at the man she so stupidly loved to within a nail of what Solancei considered 'decent', and as though resigned to her wrath, Bilan cloaked his eyes, lowering the lids to offer Iambre a simple habitual nod of sketchy compliance.

Solancei's contempt seemed to rise a notch, she couldn't help it. *Compliance could be shoved beyond a place of sunshine!*

She countered her friend's posture: narrowing her eyes a fraction more, deliberately folding her arms beneath her breasts to add her own hint of challenge, and held Iambre's eyes with the weight of her own. *If Bree wanted to go there, then let her bring it! She would not let Iambre bully her the way Bilandro Metavo allowed! She would not! The ruddy woman was insufferable!*

Resisting the urge to tap her foot, she choked back a ripe, acerbic comment and cut her gaze away to study the nails on her right hand with a little too much attention to the one that had cracked uncomfortably close to her skin this morning. *Whatever she might have said would carry no weight now.* The princess was frustrated and clearly on a roll, but Inkar'Chi strike her down here and now: the persuasion to slap her friend was becoming an itch and to avoid the development of an embarrassing scene, Solancei tucked her hands away just a little more firmly. *Oh but let her say one more word... just one...*

Yet Iambre was not blind, of course, and with a sniff of dismissal, she swivelled on her heel to 'pounce' on the safer 'option'.

"Now if enough has been said about roads and stupidity," she spat at Bilan, "then let me finish this embarrassing discussion by reminding the Captain that he currently seems *lacking!* Must I remind you that I do not

136

need to waste my time listening to excuses when results must be provided; need I remind the Captain that when I say 'hop', I expect him to perform! I am the Realm's Heiress! Surely to the Gods that guide us, I do not ask that much of you?!"

Well, Solancei thought with a slanted smile for the irony, *actually you do* - and as Bilan grew instantly stone-faced, Iambre must have realised her mistake too. But the words were out and now it was much too late for the princess to retract the sentence, just as it was finally much too late for Captain Metavo to mince his words for her 'royal' benefit.

"Oh Highness,-" the Captain intoned, eyes no longer hooded as he smiled without humour to look down on Solancei's wilful friend with a mixture of regret and restrained anger, "-as I stand before you, so you may surely command me! And, should Your Royal Highness ever demand 'jump', I will ever ask 'how high, yet know this, Highness: under no circumstances will I stand subject to this tone of discourteous abuse! Not for one moment longer!"

With apparent effort, Bilan managed to swallow some other choice comment he appeared to have in mind. Instead, clasping his right wrist hard between the fingers of the left hand, he leant slightly forward to fire off his final words with a dignified calm that could have stunned a seasoned ambassador with the level of aloof accomplishment. "So, Milady may proceed to summon me at her convenience of course, but I humbly request that she removes that would-be royal tiara that appears to be stuck in her mule-headed backside, before she moves to do so next time. Now respectfully, I bid you good eve!"

Iambre gaped like a winded sparrow but the man never noticed, and never forgetting to salute, Bilandro Metavo - *Royal Lance-Captain of the Legion and would-be fool for the indecent feelings he continued to harbour for Iambre* - turned smartly on his heel to march from their presence with just the slightest hint of a nod for Solancei as he left.

He was a braver man than she'd previously thought. That deserved some credit too.

Solancei whisked a grin from her face, momentarily wishing the man had been just as worthy of her friend in title, as he was currently proving to be in spirit.

Not Even a 'By Your Leave'

In the Captain's sudden absence, an obliterating silence traipsed across the stuffy pavilion as though sentient. Astounded, the princess gaped for several hefty breaths, a hint of untarnished surprise now modelling her face into a pretty good picture of a half-wit. *It was deservedly just.* If it had been possible, Solancei could've framed that expression for sheer extortion later, and it was almost a shame when the princess finally seemed to recall herself.

"I… I cannot believe the man's nerve!" she ventured, still slightly goggle-eyed, voice shaking. "Gods! I will have him whipped for insolence – not to mention…!"

Solancei waited patiently as her friend rambled on. As per usual she elected not to pay too much attention to the particulars said right then, for though assuredly 'a lady', Iambre also possessed a pretty temper and it seemed to mar her choice of vocabulary to the point where Solancei sometimes had to bite her lip not to break into giggles. To hear the soft profanities and awe-inspiring threats come out of Iambre was like listening to cats waxing lyrical in the dead of night: it was grossly annoying and all rather unintelligible anyway. The princess would rant and rave, but it was all blustery bravado that would never see the light of day anyway - particularly where Bilan was concerned, for this Heiress was not about to do anything, anytime soon, that might damage or otherwise endanger the man. *Unless, of course, one permitted for the possibility of her finally luring him in between her sheets one stormy night…*

Solancei gritted her teeth.

That particular mental image was one she might have done without, and a futile streak of desperation started to cipher into her at the idea. Never before had Iambre acted with such… *such promiscuous intentions.* It was like… *it was like she'd been bewitched!*

She clenched her fingers tightly around the elbows, watching the knuckles grow white. *Love was a useless, dangerous thing! It lost you sight of self and surroundings; of what mattered! But Iambre mustn't lose herself in that trap! She wouldn't let such a thing happen to her friend if she could help it, but-*

She wiped the frown of concern from her face before Iambre could spy it and make comment. Beneath it was still her anger at this escalating drama and she felt it twist her belly. *What did it matter that she knew Iambre wasn't really angry with any of them? What did it help that she knew Iambre was simply only ranting against the fate that bound her; against the destiny, which she didn't relish, yet could do nothing to change?*

As her friend, Solancei could relate. *But Gods… she could never tell a soul about any of this! Not one…*

Iambre's otherwise perfectly pent-up emotions needed an outlet – *she understood this too* - but it made none of them proud when Iambre behaved like this. It was a sodden excuse for what could only be described as thoroughly 'ugly behaviour' - and since Iambre had never had 'this kind of problem' before, it was probably an understatement to say that she didn't cope well. *Gods, but the two of them had never been so at odds over anything before either. Never!*

Solancei swallowed, wondering how long she herself would be able to cope. *The anger in her core told her: not long…*

Rounding on her, rousing the five layers of fine soft fabric in her wide sleeves, Iambre threw out a hand in the general direction that Bilan had taken, and the abrupt action severed Solancei's musings.

"Anyway, how dare he bolt from my presence without as much as a 'by your leave'?" Iambre's normally pleasant voice rose uncomfortably with every syllable, "I have not yet finished with him! I mean, does he literally not see that I have not yet finished with him?"

"Well, *you* might not be finished with *him,-*" Solancei offered neutrally, though with a touch of obliterating dryness, before she cleared her throat, "-but I guess... I guess that he's very much finished with you... *Milady.*"

Hearing her tone, Iambre's scowl deepened. "I beg your pardon?!"

"Oh Bree, I think you heard me well enough,-" Solancei sighed, breaking loose a hand to gesture with frustration, "-and I think it abundantly clear why he left."

"Verily?" Iambre enquired in a deceptively smooth tone that seemed to jar with her crystal stare. "And what would my Shield know about such matters? *You?* A mere handmaiden - whom I might add - seems incapable of showing an interest in anyone of the opposite gender! Gods, Lancei, it seems I barely know you anymore! Seems that you have become my mother rather than my friend, these passing moons."

Her mother?! Solancei bit back a splutter of denial and felt the anger burn a little brighter, but Iambre didn't notice.

"Are you jealous?" The princess carried on, "Is that it? Tell me, because I cannot understand you! You're more my 'conscience-in-waiting' than anything else these days, but don't let your persuasions ruin others, please! The way you so persistently act sends me mad! Either lend me your support or else I might find myself no longer able to entertain your company quite so frequently. Gods, to think of it: why should I even value the insight of a would-be spinster anyway? I am really not sure of our friendship... in this, or... or in everything else, for that matter!"

Jealous?! Would-be spinster?! Linking her arms back up a little tighter, Solancei flashed Iambre a stare that might have served to further-paralyse sheet-ice. The words were hurtful; she'd heard it all before though, and suddenly the princess' childish behaviour made her sad even as it grated on her nerves. The callous verbal attack was uncalled for, but she could live with that for it seemed but the desperate snap of a puppy toying for attention, and Solancei let a soft touch of coruscating Veranto oxidize the intended slights to help them fall unheeded. *It left but the 'ranting'. Much she'd take, but the ranting...*

Iambre was Princess of Ostravah! She had everything! *What more could she possibly want?* Certainly not the blossoming of this... this 'love' - because this thing that her friend pretended to feel for the Captain...

Well, it was not real. It mustn't be real!

Resisting the urge to shift her feet, Solancei pulled a face.

"Bree, you are being irrational," she began in a tempered voice, "and if I know so very little indeed, at least I do know that love is a ridiculous feeling! However, Captain Metavo does not deserve this wrath of yours. He is only performing his duty, you know! Don't waste your time."

"Well, if he is so dutiful, how come I barely see the man?" Iambre complained, "How come he sends others to see me? How come he reports on our progress as randomly as the strength of tomorrow's wind? How come I am Princess and yet I am the last one to learn of these things? It is intolerable! He should report properly to me! Every day! About ridiculous delays and... And other stuff!"

Iambre spun from her friend's knowing eyes and kicked a golden pillow across the temporary layers of sumptuous Esardan rugs.

"We need the wheel fixing! Again! At this rate we will never reach Zanzier, and Gods, Lancei, I tire of this nomadic existence, of tents and dust!

Gods, perhaps we might as well just travel the *Wilderness* - I hear the gnats cannot survive the arid conditions. That ruddy city is still weeks away, it might as well be months for all the progress we make!" Iambre glared over her trim shoulder at Solancei, daring her friend to say aloud what they both knew, but would not speak of in the light of day.

Solancei returned the look and bit down on the stripping reply that lingered ready on the tip of her tongue. They'd also had *this* conversation before and it never ended well. She felt a headache coming on, and since she was unwilling to cross 'swords' with Iambre for the rest of the evening, she offered her unhappy friend a tight smile of diplomacy.

"Princess," she entreated, pushing an escaped wave of dark hair back from her forehead, "I hear you – never fear – I do. And first of all, just so we're clear: let me tell you that I don't think the Wilderness will be the answer you are looking for; then let me be blunt: we both know what's really the problem here, don't we, hmm? Now whether you think me nothing but your simple Shield, the facts behind my words will not alter! All I am advising is that you shouldn't blame 'the messenger' for denying himself something that your own shortfall would damn him for."

Iambre's jaw tightened in contrite anger then, but Solancei suspected it was only because she had hit the spot. *'Do not ask the man to act against his code, even if he clearly, desperately wants to'.* Those were the words she might as well have said to the princess, but her uncensored version seemed too callous perhaps - and she could hold her tongue when needed.

Why did Iambre persist though? In Solancei's opinion, she should simply admit that she'd blundered and then she could 'free' Bilan instead of holding him 'prisoner' in this continuous web of tangled hope and sworn duty. Iambre could just not do it, though. *It was a worrying development.*

Solancei drew a breath to staunch her lingering frustration. *Yes, Iambre had a point: the Captain was avoiding her but there could be no doubt as to the reasoning behind his actions. Iambre wanted him to 'report' all right! 'Report' all night if 'princess-smitten' had her own way!*

Solancei felt her slow prickly anger trail back into life with languid ease, the link to the State of Veranto once more shifted from her grasp without her feeling it. That worried her, though currently not as much as Iambre. *Why should her friend push the Captain so mindlessly for something that would ultimately ruin them both? Why the refusal to see good sense?*

Eyeing Iambre's set features through her lashes, Solancei bit her bottom lip and exhaled carefully. *Were Iambre to continue, then it would only be a matter of time before Bilan 'obliged'.* She had seen him look at the Princess; she wasn't naive. Just like everyone else in this flecking realm, the damned Captain desired her friend, all right - yet unlike anyone else, this particular man would not have his advances rebuked if he should decide to go on another 'royal quest'. *It could be covered up.* She'd do that and worse for Iambre. However, should the unlikely couple throw rules and honour to the wind, Solancei feared there wouldn't be enough insults in the world to prise a wedge between them after. *And then what?*

Would the fool be able to let Iambre go when the time came that he must? *And would Iambre even let him?*

Solancei was weary of wondering what would become of the man – of what would become of them all - if he should succumb to Iambre's wily wishes.

"You know that you should let him go." Speaking with quiet force, she broke the oppressive silence.

As expected, the truth did not bear up well. Iambre stiffened for a heartbeat, right before she shot Solancei an animated look of warning. "For the love of our friendship: do not go there, Lancei!"

"But you jeopardise everything,-" Solancei felt her control slipping, "-the realm, the future, yourself – and for what? Fleeting fancies and hopeless desires! You always told me to be honest with you! Well, now I am! You know it cannot happen. Be thankful the man has a sound measure of personal restraint or we'd all be in the soup!"

Looking indignant, Iambre drew herself up, her celestial nose somewhat ruining the self-righteous effect. "But we haven't done anything wrong, Lancei!"

"No you haven't-" Solancei retorted, unwilling to let the Heiress' defensive tone touch her, "–but you will! And I guess I am but your 'ignorant friend and Shield' but tell me: are you fully prepared to face the consequences? Rats Iambre, can't you comprehend this is something I seek to protect you from? Just lift your stubborn daffodil out of the trenches for a moment and listen, would you!"

For a heartbeat Iambre's expression turned morbidly hostile, then she stalked to stand face to face with her friend and life-shield. Measuring Solancei with narrow tolerance, she drew her shoulders back like a man and it seemed the air bristled with pent-up emotion as they stared at each other, disagreement fighting friendship, new priorities clashing: in the silence a dozen words of apology dying on each breath. Eye-to-eye, nose-to-nose, Iambre made as if to speak, only in that very moment, Palea entered the pavilion, laden with a wide wooden tray bearing teapots and cups, and Iambre's mouth snapped shut, a softening measure of compromise evaporating from her face. It made Solancei feel like she died a little inside, but she too remained silent.

Pushing at the silk and canvas to navigate through the opening with a tiny mutter of complaint for the skill it took to perform the action without accident, Palea had yet not realised the tension and simply proceeded to balance her assorted teas towards the nearest table. *She was about a pace removed when she had the sudden wherewithal to finally sense the loaded atmosphere. Then...*

As might have been predicted, surprise blossomed on Palea's face, slashed the next moment by a hint of nervous indecision as she paused mid-step.

Never one to interrupt, mostly – *probably* - for fear that she'd get shouted at by Solancei, the simpering handmaiden seemed to acquire an instant aura of perturbed distress as she lingered, battling this unexpected challenge. In truth she would usually want to make herself scarce whenever the princess and Solancei drew into one of their verbal clashes, only this time she was caught in the middle, and Solancei noted the other woman's already cramped hold on the tray intensify as she dithered a moment, then cleared her throat as if to remind them of her presence.

Solancei turned her attention away, choosing to ignore her younger colleague. She was still centred on Iambre and did not wish to add another fatality to their already escalating situation, but it was most likely the jarring of porcelain cups rather than Palea's actual presence that finally seemed to penetrate Iambre's veneer and break their stalemate.

With a strange look, Iambre exhaled sharply and shifted a fraction to resume a stiff smile.

"You Lancei," she began in low, haughty tones, "You, I love like a sister, but do not presume to tell me what to do in this matter, do you hear! We've had these discussions before and they are beginning to bore me! Just because you've decided to remain above anyone's affections, doesn't mean

146

that we're all meant to be like that. You hate 'love' - but your feelings on the matter do not mirror mine! Your misfortune was unfair; and yes, you got scarred, but people are dead and gone, and we go-"

Skirts flaring, Solancei chose that very moment to spin on her heel and abandon her friend.

"Hey!" Iambre shouted as if to halt her or bring her pause to return, but ignoring her, Solancei proceeded to march from the black and green pavilion without another word.

Something grey seemed about to strangle her; she felt sick: her skin clammy, her heart pierced by something that threatened to floor her. She had just time to note Palea's look of stricken, scandalous surprise, then she was at the tent-flap. *The anger was pushing forth now; belatedly. She fed it. It was better than the alternative; better than thoughts of Sandborn, long lost to her!*

With an aggressive shove, she pushed at the heavy canvas. She wasn't wearing her veil but she didn't care as she thrust herself between the two statutory guards to exit.

On the inside she was shivering from the shock of emotions she'd thought long buried and just like Bilandro Metavo, she flat-out refused to stay a moment longer in the presence of that *'thing'* who claimed to be her friend. Somehow Iambre seemed as blind to reason as ever, but when she began raking up the past, Solancei had to bow out – which was probably just as well, for she had little desire to pursue their 'disagreement' in front of a gossip like Palea. The news that the princess was in love with the captain of her retinue would travel within a day then and she'd be damned if she'd kept the flecking secret only to have it spread as carelessly as dung on a field in less than a heartbeat. *So… here you are…*

She shook herself of the haunting experience and just walked. She was on a circuit towards the horses...

Composing herself a little when a nearby groom cast her a curious look, even from afar, Solancei drew a deep breath and donned her usual 'mask' to say 'do not approach' as she ploughed a path through the loose dust and dry grasses. Once again, the feeling of déjà-vu returned to her – strong enough to weigh her steps with peculiar anxiety that did not stem from Iambre at all. Still, in lieu of lingering thoughts on the words of her and Iambre's fallout, she didn't particularly mind. She needed distance. Otherwise, she might cry. The State of Veranto eluded...

But how could Iambre drag up the past to fling it at her like a weapon? She blinked, letting her umbrage dry the tears before they could do more than threaten. *Gods' death! This was beyond fair! Beyond-*

A disconcerting shiver shimmied down her back though she had no reason to be cold: the evening was still pleasantly tempered for the season and she was well-attired!

'Now as well as then', her mind seemed to whisper in odd reminder - and again, she shivered.

'Now, as well as then, you'd worn no leathers on this day', her mind echoed; taunting her – and Solancei resisted the urge to hug herself as she marched on. *Peculiar was maybe too kind a word...*

Solancei's Memoirs

The Province of Tarléon.
Ocean's End.
Autumn of 780 P. C. W.

Do you dream?

If you do – and I am semi-reliably informed that we all do, though we cannot always recall – then you will already know that just as with the 'accident', there are dreams – and then there are 'Dreams'.

The first are of the maniacal kind where you must save the rabbit with the green patch on its cheek before the clock strikes full, or something bad will happen – but of course, it never does, because you are privileged enough to escape slumber before it all goes north, east, west, whatever. *However, as for the second kind…*

The second kind is so vivid that you can taste the sweat of fear on the air, it's so detailed that you could spot the individual hairs of a wolf from half a mile away and still understand that distance is relative and danger not always approaching from where you think it should. However, now take this idea of 'reality' and multiply it tenfold. *Would you be surprised to learn that there is yet another kind of 'dream'?*

Well, I imagine that maybe you would not be all that surprised – and so I'm going to attempt to relay what happened next in my parents' carriage, but it might make small sense: I for one have taken years to understand and it still barely adds up to anything of coherent explanation, but… but…

Well I will try to describe this peculiar incident because you might find it interesting – and in a sense, I believe these confessions cathartic, so here goes…

I found myself in my parents lost coach, the spear in my head gone on a wink as though only imagined, and I wondered then if I was indeed dreaming, but because I was so lucid, it seemed impossible not to consider the event real.

That of course, was to be the greatest re-occurring trick with these vision-like fits, I suppose. And from the very first, to my credit, I was aware that something didn't quite fit reality just the same; I was aware, because my perception was off: no longer two dimensional, but somehow trapped in a furrow, way beyond that.

Hah, so did I not tell you it got strange? That it got twisted? Well, just you wait. It gets better yet, but I unexpectedly find myself in need of a cup of wine first. And fair enough, all considering it may not be viewed the best timing, but when did I ever concern myself with common opinions?!

Solancei

Dreams of Jackals

As she walked, however, Solancei's mind finally seemed to go quiet for her anger was slowly burning itself out. It was almost a comfort - but for the fact that the throbbing in her head was replacing it, increasing her desire for solitude. Topping this came Iambre's reference to her past, which seemed to gnaw at her insides now, and to compensate for the sudden chill in her bones, she pulled up the loose swag of fabric that fell across the back of her shoulders to serve an impromptu hood if desired.

Drawing it low over her eyes, she stared at the toes of her boots, lengthening her strides to suit her mood. *'Just like then',* she put her discomfort down to being tired, because... *because she was?*

Again the oddly bizarre idea flickered through her mind that *'now'* – just as *'then'* – she'd worn no leathers and for a moment her mind seemed to spin as she had to glance down her attire just to reassure herself. But of course she was appropriately dressed as she'd known she would be, the mauve and lilac swatches of her wide skirts flaring, providing a pleasing compromise between functional and delicate. *In this outfit, she could perform every duty needed, even the intricate moves of Kizano.*

Solancei pushed at the notion. *Shield or no, she had little intention of going back to Iambre any time tonight – so watch her Belanzia'Cha, Goddess of Clarity! And yet...*

The metal segments that made up the 'Tears of Mourning' danced and bounced against the layers of her dress in rhyme with her steps, raising second thought.

Like the prized necklace she wore hidden under her shift, the metal belt was a reminder of her duty; a reminder that whatever else might happen, the two of them were bound: she as Iambre's life-shield, and Iambre...

For a moment, she almost chose to return; then she thought the better of it. *Oh Gods take Iambre's foul mind and stuff it with hay!* The Princess was too well protected amidst her ring of soldiers and retainers for Solancei to be missed tonight and ignoring the stubborn reminder of the diamond-shaped links as they jingled softly, Solancei found herself crudely wondering if she mightn't just be justified doing away with Captain-flecking-Metavo!? *The Tears of Mourning would do well… A dark evening… late… he would never see the shuriken coming…*

Immediately, she snorted without mirth at her own fancy. *Easier just to draw her dagger then, but no!* Sure, she might consider doing such a thing to protect Iambre, but she could of course never kill Metavo - she was not a flecking assassin - and his feelings for Iambre aside, she actually didn't particularly mind the Captain. He seemed a good man. For a 'near-peasant' he'd risen high - and with good reason - even if he should learn to mind his duty and stop dreaming; she'd already warned him!

"Lady Solancei! My Lady, please wait! A favour if you would…?"

The shout rocked her from the contemplations of Metavo's demise and the event sprung another sensation of recognition within her. Like 'before', someone shouted her name – a man - and just like 'then', Solancei clenched her jaw, seriously considering how best to ignore the hail. It would be rude, of course, but it would hardly bother her standing; they all thought worse things about her regardless, except-

Except, perhaps, for this one…

And just as 'before', habit made her halt.

Turning, she already knew – *'now' as she had 'then'* - that she would see Bilan Metavo's lanky second-in-command and right she was. Lieutenant Commander del´Draventar was running to catch her up, waving one arm, as if to solidify her attention now that he'd made her pause. Of course she already knew his purpose, just as she knew that she'd listen to the message that was meant to excuse the 'interruption'.

Indeed, 'now' as he had been 'then', Kimonar del'Draventar was here to 'beg' of her a favour. *A favour of a few words passed on to Iambre without the incriminating use of ink or vellum. A few words to 'inform' the princess that the Captain sent her his unreserved apologies, not to mention his deepest, most sincere regrets for the recent 'incident'.*

'Oh the fool!' she had the time to think, then Kimonar caught her up.

The man was not even out of breath, but for a moment he seemed unable to speak all the same as his too-blue eyes flew across her unveiled features. Then recalling himself, he offered her an apologetic half-smile.

Of course that distracted - damn him if it wasn't quite the disarming smile he had on him, this del'Draventar, but-

She grimaced within: something that felt like embarrassment. Of course, the man was a fine soldier too, and the slight gap between his front teeth made him retain a hint of boyish charm, even when she knew for certain he had a good five years on Metavo's age. Combined with those sun-streaked highlights in his shoulder-length, sandy-coloured hair, any oaf could see he was not without appeal, but...

But maybe she truly was an idiot?

Solancei gave him a bland stare, and though he was both a Lord and a noble, she saw him hesitate. Then his composure was back.

"My Lady." With practised ease, he performed a small polite bow in deference to her status and Solancei had no choice but to also incline her head, although she did not smile back.

"Lord Lieutenant Commander. What might I do for you?"

With a subconscious gesture of discomfort, Kimonar raked a hand back through his slightly dishevelled hair as if to tidy his appearance. It made no difference - *the hair seemed to have a natural kink* – and as she had done 'before', Solancei cocked her head a fraction to study the man.

It wasn't the first time she found herself wondering just how much he might actually know about the feelings that swelled between his loyal commander and the princess. *Not much... she hoped.* And as he appeared to search for the right words, yet again she contemplated the relative ease with which she seemed to tolerate Lord Kimonar del'Draventar better than most.

"I... that is to say, Captain Metavo wishes to..." Kimonar petered off, looking ill-at-ease.

The words broke Solancei's line of thinking in two, which was just as well. She didn't have all night and she sent him a glare now, so as to say 'do not linger', because after what had just transpired and because of her odd vibes, she was just not in the mood to speak with anybody. *Indeed, not even Lord-flecking-Kimonar with his very blue eyes and very-easy smile.*

Regarding him from under the folds of her hood, Solancei nevertheless awaited his words patiently, unable to move on though she already knew what was coming: he'd deliver the apology, she'd walk back to Iambre and relay the words in a rather unflattering fashion – because that's what she'd promise to do; because she too was a fool - *of a kind* - and felt guilty – *in a fashion.* Iambre would then shatter into a hopeless mess of tears and apology, begging Solancei her forgiveness and then they'd be friends again because they never really reached a point where they weren't anyway. Then, Iambre would forget Bilan for a while whilst they laughed and nagged each other late into the night before falling asleep back-to-back on Iambre's feather mattress. The next day Captain Metavo would rake up another 'slight' - and her friend would order the detour into the Wilderness, and

Metavo - though secretly forgiven - would learn just how devious Iambre might get when slighted. *Gods! It was a crazed life…*

Suddenly wrapped in the notion of forgiveness, she felt a tiny bit more amicable as she looked at Kimonar and watched him draw breath to speak again. *Metavo should really not make his mate do this, it was-*

Her ribcage throbbed just once with a rolling pain she'd all but forgotten: a catalyst, it shattered through her reality and alarm flared. *This was not part of what she knew or remembered!*

The unreal sensation caused the Lieutenant Commander's face to waver in and out of focus before her eyes, but impossibly the man appeared indifferent to the change in her as he began to talk.

She didn't hear a word…

Breath hitching, Solancei doubled over, her vision floating strangely out of focus and time. *Del'Draventar disappeared as though enveloped in a haze, then came back into focus.*

"I would protect you!" he assured her, completely out of context; she didn't understand why, but his eyes trailed some kind of threat she could not see.

Her vision wavered again. Her body was awash with vivacious pain and her head throbbed. 'Are we under attack?' she wanted to cry, rubbing her temples and feeling worse by the beat, but a ring of steel cut back her words as del'Draventar drew his ancestral sword with an aggressive flourish.

It was too strange. She could not perceive of any danger and yet the tension was in the air, permeating her guts. *It reminded her of something else.* Something she'd once known, perhaps in a dream, but-

She couldn't seem to see properly though. There was a fog shifting over the landscape and suddenly she was afraid.

"Fall back, My Lady." Kimonar made a gesture to accentuate the advice and she obliged, meekly as though she did not know how to look after herself though part of her knew that she could.

"It's only ever a question of time. Did I not tell you?"

The menacing words sounded out of nowhere next to her ear - not del'Draventar's voice – and she startled, new fear playing hopscotch with her heart as she whirled to look for the man who'd spoken. *There were too many layers. Part of her knew this was a dream. Part of her-*

The dream seemed to pull her away from Kimonar as though it were a piece of knitting unravelling. Darkness was descending all around her, taking the Lieutenant Commander from view, deepening and eating her courage, and she couldn't seem to catch her breath all of a sudden. Somewhere far, far away, she heard the Chief yell an order to move faster, but it fluttered away like a ribbon on a breeze and suddenly she was alone and cold, the scenery draped in shadows and strange, tall buildings that looked mostly ramshackle.

Solancei spun, heartbeat soaring. She wasn't wearing comfortable skirts anymore but rather her tight, scarred leathers. She squinted, yet couldn't seem to see properly in this dusky environment. *A strange menace lurked, though.* In those too-dark corners and too-silent alleys, it seemed a thing coming to life; she knew something about to happen, but she wasn't ready...

As if fashioned out of smoke and air, the armed men were suddenly there, stalking and surrounding her, appearing from shadows as though made of shadows, which made it impossible for her to determine their features...

"You know who I am?" A voice whispered, splintering her world in fear and pain.

Where was del'Draventar when you needed him, she hazily wondered - then she doubled over, the routine act of breathing becoming an unexpected, monumental effort.

The world was spinning, as was her vision. All at once she felt colder than ice, yet hotter than fire. *The shadow-men stalked closer… a strange streak of desperation made her weak.*

She had to get away from here, but just like the earlier part of her dream, she knew she wouldn't be able to - and in that moment something moved within her head: something like the heavy cogs of a complicated invention turning to fall into place. It shifted her: the sensation knocking her mentally sideways, splitting her - and knowing a sense of displacement, Solancei fled to the deep shadows, cowardly hiding.

The men did not appear to notice though. They were focused on the woman still in their midst. *A woman wearing Solancei's leathers, raising a haitu in grim readiness…*

Another silent 'clank' seemed to resonate in her mind… *fading.* She was somewhere else, she thought… *and yet she wasn't.* Slowly the darkness seemed to lift, restoring her physical sight and the event was both familiar and strange.

She was staring at a scene set in the back-waters of Zanzier old town and unlike earlier, everything appeared to her with an aching, preternatural clarity now: without blurring; without double-vision or stars. Indeed, such was the shift that she could see yellow paint peeling off the shutter to her right, showing light green underneath; so much so that she could feel the pervasive chill in the damp air, and the rotting door panel at her back where her hand sought support. She could smell the stench of burning coal laced with wood, cheap offal, and other backyard 'perfumes' that seemed to fluctuate with every pass of blustery wind to rival Servangar's middens and worse. *Danger. There was too much danger. She'd almost made her escape; she'd run and they'd chased her to this deserted road and re-engaged their task.*

A male shout of anger made her look up from where she was sheltering.

A fight was in full flow. She watched without surprise as her own rampant form moved across the ground, but felt no connection for she was merely appraising herself like she would have some kind of strange, exotic animal worthy of interest. It sparked another sense of deja-vu but the idea lost form, the provenance shredding.

The doppelgänger was 'dancing': sparring it would appear, against several opponents - but it could not be friendly sport for the 'other her' was unarmed and moving in a way that was so familiar she didn't have to second-guess the severity of the situation.

Floating in detachment, she watched the other Solancei catch a glancing swipe of a real blade on her forearm just above her vambrace. It cut cloth and skin, it might have hurt, but the Solancei she was watching never paused as she ducked instantly left and kicked the descending blade from a second opponent's grasp with well-timed precision.

The part of her that was hiding in the shadows, heard the unfortunate man yelp in pain as his blade arched sideways to land in a shallow puddle only feet away, and for a moment she felt her arm smarting, but it was not enough to slow her now-filthy counterpart down. Sensing instead the spear aimed at her back, the fighting Solancei dropped and rolled free before the man who wielded it might thrust it home. It was a calculated move of course and as she flowed back to her mud-coated feet, the sword from the puddle became hers.

Another swordsman sailed past, extending his aim but still managing to miss her and in a blur Solancei with the sword reverted her action, dropped low to spin like a skater on one knee, simultaneously slashing the man's hamstrings with her new acquisition.

He issued a harsh cry going down, mud splattering high as he crashed. Another man's boot rushed towards her almost at the same time. She shifted and sought to evade, yet her reaction wasn't fast enough, perhaps the ground too slow...

The kick connected squarely with her gut to send her gasping like a fish out of water and she folded, going down alongside the man she'd only just cut. *Red-tinted grime squished under her hands... blood?... not hers...*

Solancei in the shadows cursed warning that went unheard as someone else moved in to kick her other-self before she had a chance to gather her wits sufficiently to scramble from the contact but the ground was slick, the assailant slipped, and the intended harm was deflected off her leg without any real damage, and still...

Much to her surprise, the Solancei who was watching felt the blossoming pain trail up her own limb like a roving grass fire, even as her twin on the ground pushed through the same pain with a strength rooted in desperation to get back up. Knowledge of the detail arose something in her. *She was exhausted but she had to move: had to get up - or she'd be worse off than dead!*

The thought had only just registered when something else hit her, landing her first one, then another crushing blow to her lower left ribcage. It penetrated her disembodied form just as she saw her physical twin crumble to the ground for the second time.

Then pain connected. *In an instant, her eyesight seemed to sharpen exponentially as she looked upon a scenery below, caught it would seem, in the grips of chaos.* In contrast to everything that was happening, one man trailing magenta blood was dragging himself through the filth on the ground, clearly in order to escape the fight, but other men-of-arms-and-determination were rushing forth; closing in.

Another foot connected with her chin and she jackknifed as something hit her twice in the guts sending a savage blaze of conflicting pain through her body.

She pushed away, still her arm was kicked from under her. A newcomer; a man, tall - cropped blond hair plastered to the skull by rain - sported a dull-lacquered blue haitu in one hand as he straddled her counterpart on the ground, unconcerned by grime and water. *She knew him: fear lacerated deep, cutting reserves…*

Her breath hitch within her: bones cracked; it was unreal; it made her whole; it broke her into a thousand pieces. She was trapped, stuck, the pain like finely-knitted lace laid out within her body. She could move but it seemed a futile thing; the cold mud was inches deep under her cheek, releasing an earthy, rotten stench that somehow meant nothing though she felt her fingers digging for purchase. A forlorn lost shoe, half-trodden into the muddy ground, formed a strangely compelling picture a little to the right, but it was incidental. *She didn't seem capable of resistance: she couldn't feel her jaw. She knew she must move, do something, but-*

She sensed the man bend even lower to whisper something in her ear before straightening back upright again, laughing briefly as he issued a string of orders she only half-heard.

"You should have yielded." The words seemed to echo. *"You should have yielded, witch."*

Feelings she'd forgotten, clawed through her; emotions swarmed. Then her perception lurched anew as someone yanked her upright, the action losing her the hard-won blade and Solancei would have emptied her stomach then but for the unexpected, abrupt change in her awareness. *Something seemed to stir in her – pulling her from the dream and suddenly there was no longer any stinking mud or men. Instead the darkness was back, her injuries were real, and-*

Somehow she came to a little, then. There was no light. Still, something had a feel of reality about it and confusion burned through her. In less than a handful of breaths, notions of anger towards Iambre warred with the picture of Lord Kimonar standing before her, delivering his message, which in turn warred with the plummeting despair still very much with her from having been told to yield. *And there was something about that... something-*

Solancei swallowed rising bile. She found it hard to centre on a single thought suddenly: they just did not seem to stick in her head. A hungry coldness was gnawing within her bones, her hands were numb and still lashed together, and her head was resting against the rough surface of a clammy floor where a raised ridge dug into her right temple, invigorating an already throbbing headache.

She'd fled the jackal fight and then-

With the echoes of her bizarre lifelike visions still floating in her mind, Solancei licked dry lips and shifted her body just a fraction before she was robbed of effort. Like earlier, it was making her retch but she was too dry inside; *too-*

A snippet of memory crashed into her. *The Regulators... they'd taken her down! Or rather... her cheating opponent had!*

In the place of panic, a basic kind of survival instinct kicked in and following her own mental advice, she let herself rest against the rocky floor willing her lungs to draw-in shallow breaths only: one unfulfilling gasp at a time.

The Veranto was eluding her, she remembered, just as another instinctual groping left her feeling rather like a mere 1st year Apprentice - a level she'd passed at the age of just nine autumns. *It was a hard comparison for her to consider, let alone to admit to. She needed the relief the Veranto could bring her now; needed the calm and strength she might harvest! What was happening to her that it did not work?! If she could but reach forth to forge the usual link, she needn't be in this pain! She could banish it easily, before...*

Her frustration grew then, but she was powerless to change it. Her eyes felt puffy, her face stiff and her throat raw as though she were coming down with a chill; she was thirsty and-

"You should have yielded." The words fluttered in her head like scatty birds. *She knew the man who'd done this to her. Knew his name. He had broken her ribs. He...*

She shut her eyes tightly. *Her wrists tied up; men holding her upright beyond need – her lashing out: head reeling from a kick; a haitu of sleek arrow-wood shattering bone upon impact... hurting her! A punch... hurting her! A flare of pain... then another...*

Solancei brought her numb fingertips to the limp weave of the crusted fraying hole in her cotton sleeve. The sword had cut her just below the elbow joint, she was lucky it had not severed ligaments, but it stung, had bled and dried enough to merge the wound with fabric...

She placed a numb hand against the sleek surface of her leather breeches. *Like one of Ina Uttorian's card houses on the brink of collapse, her memory lingered on the cusp of disaster – then...*

The truth about Simaro and the jackal fight slammed home like the explosion of colours that had borne her under in due result upon receiving that final well-aimed blow to the head which had kicked her into the abyss of oblivion.

She flinched within herself as if she might avoid the blow. Simaro had allowed the Regulator with the whistle to provide that 'service' though it hadn't truly served them then: she'd already been down; on her knees but unlikely to get back up. She recalled seeing the flash of the blade, recalled seeing it swing towards her and feeling the rush of terror and resignation as she thought herself about to be executed - only he'd hit her with the back, not the edge…

She tentatively brushed numb fingers to the crusty elongated swelling along the right side of her temple that felt as though it might split her skull. Absurdly, she vaguely wondered if she still had all her teeth, her tongue flowing to investigate then halting the move. *It was best not to care. Something had gone terribly wrong. Terribly…*

Solancei felt her remainder of strength leeching from her a little more by the heartbeat. *She feared she had not enough left of any virtue to face the truth - not enough to face what might come of this – and yet she'd have to. She'd surely have to!*

A Gift of Foresight

"Mama, the pretty lady is dead and the blue-haired Mshai is injured!"

The shout escaped before the girl's unseeing eyes had lost their glazed reflection and returned to the darkened room in which she resided for her daily exercises. Instant comprehension of disaster brought with it a heartfelt concern, which spread thickly through her like the unfurling tendrils of a fast-growing bindweed. *Decorum would be shattered but she sidestepped concern.*

"Mama, are you here?" she quested, more subtly, though her voice retained the slightly higher pitch than usual. "Mama?"

The girl blinked, hoping to clear her mind but the images stuck, the talons of her talent not releasing as they should. *Blood... there was too much blood.*

"Mama!" Panic stalking her breath, she didn't even try to withhold anxiety this time. Sometimes she could not get back from these 'quests' – she'd settled her mind as she'd been taught, but she was in too deep; she was too 'invested - which was what became of those Talents who could not remain objective: to those who began to care too much, or started feeling personally invested. The girl knew she was guilty on all accounts, she'd not meant it to be like that. *No, never like that, but-*

"Mama, please!" The urgent timbre seemed to carry squeakily shrill now. It was unbecoming – but so was seeing things that were not true and still allowing them to hook their fabricated tendrils into your third eye, so much so that it threatened permanent trance. *She needed an anchor.*

"Mama!"

A part of her – the part that occupied this chamber physically – cringed at this other break with decorum – yet the part that contained vision and displacement didn't care one fig-encrusted, sweet-pickled pear how much her actions would jolt the refined ideas of propriety and tact. *Was this a test?* Fumbling blindly for a hand that wasn't there, she felt herself shaking with a sudden wealth of emotions much beyond the usual scope.

Her mother was not there!

The fear of insight found refinement hard to deal with and the idea of a deliberate trial seemed even worse. *Dear Maker… she needed an anchor. They were right. She must be ill somehow, but she did not feel it.*

Empathy of the most serene, severe degree threatened to strangle her - more so this time than ever before, and for all that she *did* know; for all of her five decades of schooling - she still hadn't developed the scope to deal with these rouge attacks on her own, because her 'gift - *her 'sacred inheritance'* - did not usually manifest quite so.. *so vividly.*

The girl blinked, fighting an illness that she didn't quite comprehend. They told her she was too young for this… *this depth of Affinity,* but her mother believed them wrong. Her mother believed her, not them, because her mother had borne witness! *Wish that the Chief of Vectors could see her now though: the Watchéran's daughter reeling, blinded, on the cusp of vomiting, on the edge of passing back into the life of a vision that apparently held no place in the landscape of time…*

A gift, a curse; a curse, a gift! *So much blood…*

Feeling the senses suck at her as though she was trapped in a quackmire that wanted to drag her to the bottom in a suffocating embrace from which she'd never return, she shook her head hard so that the multiple falls of her earnings jangled. *Hers! This was her present. Her now; her time! What was not of her world must retract: the blood must retract, for that was not of her world!*

Expelling a gasp of relief for the subtle parting in the veil of fogs encircling her mind, the girl repeated her mantra over and over and felt her sight shift further towards reality. *The blood was turning pink, fading, greying in the grass that was losing its lush hues.* Slowly, so very slowly, the crystals of her focus came into view underneath – an inlay of an image like that of a powerful Elemental almost manifesting. She trapped the image in her mind and it solidified. The gold filigree tray came next, *solidifying*, then the low bow-legged cedar tree table with the Maze inlays of enamel and ivory, *solidifying* – and then finally, the far wall with the inverted spirit map and the Pyramid of Towers and the Five Paths of Persuasion.

She shuddered in relief. *If she could shake herself off this illness, the Chief of Vectors predicted she might one day rise to the 7th Tier: mercifully, prescient skills were not her only affinity…*

The girl raced her gaze from the wall, unsettled by thoughts of a future she'd never predict for herself though others already had, but her personal emotions helped. Her head was blending back into the right reality now; into the world in which she belonged.

It made her aware again of her own heartbeat and body - as if it somehow had helped to think of the possibility of a real scenario and future, rather than one of 'supposed' volatile make-belief.

She shivered with the memory in her head, still warm as newly-formed dough, but it had no power now. *She'd escaped.*

Attention now fully on the twinkling small shards bathing in the bowl before her, she drew her mind further home, inhaling the familiar, much-loved scent of cinnamon incense and burned caramel. Mama made sure the cones of delicious fragrance were always kept lit whenever her daughter occupied her quiet workroom, since it had been known to be one of the anchors that would sometimes help her stay connected to reality, and the girl frowned, realising that today it had not been the deciding factor in her success – *she had.*

For a moment the achievement left her stunned. *Her mother had decided to test her and she'd risen to the challenge?*

Would Nafretiri have gleaned an insight prior to this that her first daughter was going to have one of her perverse 'events' or had it simply happened in coincidence? Had Mama seen that this would be the day where she'd finally no longer be needed by her daughter?

With the ringing questions in the back of her head, the girl clung to the mundane sight of her workroom. The ascetic décor, the reed door-screen, the cream walls – as smooth as their millennia-old workmanship still allowed – rendered bare and without ornaments; the high-set rectangular openings that allowed shafts of light, but not direct sun.

The hazy beams slanting across the chamber softened the atmosphere in a way that was designed to promote tranquillity and as she watched the inevitable tiny specks of dust hang near motionless in the still air, she finally relaxed.

A 'gift' they called it. A 'gift'.

Mostly she concurred – except for the odd times where her visions brought her ill-tidings; oh and except for the odd times when she got 'trapped': where she couldn't seem to break away at will until 'relinquished' by the vision. It happened to others too, but not this… *this invalid twist of the imagination that would conjure up insights only into these pseudo-events - that in spite of their severity - remained unsubstantiated by both the Council, as well as the ancient Tapestry.*

Feeling weary as ever after one of her episodes, she reached slowly for the cup of water next to the now purely decorative bowl of spelled-shards on the low table. It was odd to think of the power she was able to derive from their presence, yet stranger still why she lost control of a situation that wasn't ever going to be real.

She drank with shaking hands, already taxed thinking what they would have to say about this newest addition to her now rather eclectic collection of 'tales'. She was the daughter of the Watchéran; the King. The Council for Historic Preservation was of course both too practised and too polished to offend her sensibilities, and they were indeed also too wise to risk offending their Lord and Protector by calling it what they really thought to her face, but she knew what they whispered each time she left. *Lies, they agreed. The Best-Loved Daughter of the Sabén-Heshep, Her Esteemed Highness Ankh'Sheriti-Nefer'Kemnebit, was inventing lies for her personal amusement and droll gratification.*

She would that they were right. *If only they were right!*

Nefer'Kemnebit drank again, her hands still quivering. Staring at the unassuming shards, pale and colourless beneath the clear fluids, she felt a subtle pull within before the new ripple scarred the surface. *She had a moment to blink in surprise - the shards seemed to melt and blend now, the contents becoming murky liquid silver...*

She appeared to topple towards the offered sight once more, vision and boundaries blurring to open up a path along something inbetween. Eyes and mind-twisting under strain to resist, she drew back, but the pull only intensified: the silver swivelled, becoming solid, drowning out her work chamber, leaving her instead within the gently-rising grassy lands that wavered like pond-grass in her mind. The bowl blurred last, a new world solidifying...

The clunk as the cup of water hit the alabaster flagstones was the cue that she'd dropped it and it pinged across her awareness, awakening her to the new danger. In the effort to avert it, she pinched her own arm. The room returned. Flimsy like a voile. She pinched her arm again. *Subtle pain; merciful Maker defend her but her 'gift' still pulled. She could smell the salty tang of blood. The fighting had been brief, but fierce, and the dead-*

Vision wavered... one world superimposing itself over that of her own, then almost floating from reach again. *The blood was everywhere: on the ground, on her hands, on her clothes. She could feel the rapidly-cooling stickiness all over her like a sheen of perspiration. It was in her hair, her nostrils, the taste was in the back of her throat, polluting her breath. It was unbearable to her, and the agony in her heart... It was her spirit crippling, then dying.*

The girl shook her head, swaying in her seat. *No. No, it had not crippled her! She was in her work chamber, within the palace complex. She was in her own body, drawing in smells of cinnamon and dry hazy air.* She knew this, and yet there was an urgency within her. A need to see as much as this - and more - because this was a terrible mistake and it must never come to pass.

"Mama?!" Nefer'Kemnebit heard her own fear and it spread like little pin pricks of ice all over her body. *She could not withstand this. It was pulling her in again and she had to get away but-*

From the corner of her eye, like a transcript over another, she saw the Mshai through the eyes of another. *On the ground... Wrong... And her sister!*

No!

"Mama! I need you!" *She needed an anchor.* "Mama!"

And still her workroom remained empty.

She sprang from the cushioned egg-shaped seat she'd been curled in, her feet pushing against the edge of the cedar table, nearly upending it as

169

her disregard and panic set the silver mirror in the bowl swirling and the liquid splashing over the edge of the golden filigree.

She didn't care. Not even if part of her knew it would earn her Weaver Ti-Anakit-Suh's wrath, but she didn't care-

Emotions rose up: overwhelming; drowning...

On her feet, for a moment she wavered. *Numb yet tingling with life.*

Confusion followed. The spelled-shards was strewn across the cedar, glinting gently with the moisture that had 'stilled' with them, but though the focus was broken, there was too much still within her. Grief, disbelief, fear, betrayal, or...

Or was that the emotions of the lady in her vision? Confused as two lives intertwined she gazed down. The alabaster floor was replaced with trampled grasses and once-spindly, now-broken meadow flowers already wilting. Her hands were still shaking but they looked strange - *not hers?* - fingers slender, but not weak: the fingers of an adult; fingers besmirched with blood upon skin much paler than her own...

Nefer stumbled a few blind steps in the general direction of the screen door she prayed to the Maker would still be there. *She needed an anchor...* her palms were sticky with blood. *Blood, not hers! Her sister's... An anchor... Why- Why her sister?*

She gagged for air. *Sick! Merciful Alérathnar, this might kill her. She felt sick...*

Incredulity warred with love, confusion with animosity. She wanted to pick up her discarded weapon and ram it through the Mshai all the way to the hilt. Only she couldn't move and he was already dying.

Her heart contracted; the grief ripping her. She loved him and yet he'd betrayed them all. Why? Someone was approaching. She heard their voices mix in argument. The voices of angry men. They meant nothing to her and yet she recognised one - on the ghost of a nightmare and the memories of pain, she remembered...

Fear unknown to the girl herself, shot through the woman she'd 'become'; the emotion so piercing, so instant, that it separated vision from reality far better than anything she might have attempted by herself.

Swaying by the wall, Nefer pushed for it to stop. Already, she'd seen more than she could bear. She didn't want to 'go back'! Sudden tears pressed as a hollow horror of something undefined lingered in her core. *One moment she'd felt the hot sun on her face; next, she'd tasted the dust in her mouth from the grit in the air thrown up with the careless pace and reckless abandon she'd fought the enemy to get through. The strain of killing one of the Venzoians had almost wrenched muscle and tendon apart before the natural flow of action- and horse-combined had seen her free of the 'thing', and the dull ache remained in her right arm, throbbing.*

Massaging her limb though she knew it was not her injury to bear, Nefer pulled back the screen and let it bang shut as she exited the workroom. The long hallway beyond was cool – she was behind tons of marble, fathoms thick, the intentional natural insulator against the outdoor heat - and she savoured the relief, if not the lack of people.

Real or not, what she'd seen today had shocked her. She needed real life around her right now: she needed her Mama, the water boy, servants, anyone...

Nefer frowned, then resolutely marched down the corridor, her flat hide sandals slapping forlornly at the pristine floor. Like most spaces reserved for work of the optical or pre-science related nature, the corridor remained minimally embellished to prevent distractions but doors topped by personal sigils or identifiers broke the monotony at regular intervals, their heavy frames and functional lintels all polished to the same refined perfection that had raised a rich lustre in the pale quarried rock throughout the entire wing. She knew that there'd be people at work within some of these rooms; knew that they would come to her aid regardless of convenience, should she raise alarm and cry distress, but it was frowned upon - another breach in decorum that her mother would not condone. And besides: she felt better now and realised she did not want to share her present state with strangers.

She shuddered, understanding how near to a mistake she'd almost come. In habit, as a deflection, she wanted to run her hand over her shaven head, yet refrained upon reflecting that though she might be bald, Ti-Anakit-Suh had only just renewed the complex runes of benediction and protection upon her skin. *She was not supposed to rub them until the gold had settled...*

Still, the stubbles of her rapidly-growing hair were already itching though they are now yet visible; somehow it felt worse today than usual: intensifying till the urge became unbearable.

She shook herself, deliberately turning her mind to something much worse, then. A sure thing, it dulled the itch, then killed it

Would the Council believe her this time? Always before, they'd dismissed her on the grounds of what-was-known, on the grounds of the 'discrepancies', and she wished she was allowed to see the strands of the Tapestry for herself. *Just once. To make sure.* But she was not old enough, or learned enough, or enough of anything.

"Well," they'd say to her Mama, *"of course the Best-loved Daughter is beyond gifted – that is beyond dispute - but her ability does not rival the Tapestry. Nothing does. She must first mature."*

Nefer drew a breath: felt the energy seeping from her steps. She'd have to talk to her mother about this. Today there'd been a breakthrough – even with the rouge vision and the slight hitch that had sent her running, there had been a change in her, and as she thought about it, she feared the Council and the Chief of Vectors wrong. Plenty of people saw things that never amounted to anything, but not she! Somehow they'd have to petition the Council to re-appraise her situation. *Somehow it was important that they did not give up.*

Reaching the familiar cross section in the corridor, Nefer ignored the chiselled ciphers above the giant lintels and turned left. She knew this side of the Esoteric City like the back of her hand and needed no reference to directions. The corridor she entered was likewise empty of people but it was flanked by ornamental obsidian statues and draping vines twisting from the raised gardens outside through the narrow, open rectangles twenty feet above. A chirp and a flash of wing caught her eye and she saw the flash of blue plumage as a tiny raptor swooped to hunt a fat black scarab with the grace she'd often heard ascribed to the Dragons of times now turned to dust.

She looked away. The exit was ahead: a large unadorned opening bearing neither door nor fence; she was five paces removed when the red-nosed lizard hissed at her, ruby eyes and jewelled collar flashing as it raised quivering quills in indignant alarm.

Nefer smiled benignly, then paused.

"Seih-rahrat it's me. Stop being so touchy." she berated the large squat animal, plucking a meandering, plumb beetle from the nearest vine and throwing it at the impromptu guard who caught it deftly with its prehensile tongue and did not even crunch once before gulping the treat down.

It made her glance around. *If the lizard was here, Weaver Ti-Anakit'Suh would not be far, but what about her mother?*

Drawing a steadying breath, she took a moment to run both her hands across the slightly creased pleats of her pale-cotton, knee-length dress.

Smoothing it would do nothing to reverse the effects of her morning in front of the viewing bow, but it served well to placate her urgency - and it dawned on her that if she wanted anyone to take her seriously, she'd have to act accordingly. *Straightening her clothes like an adult was only a small thing but it was a start.* Mama was usually not forgiving of slack appearances, nor of Nefer's often-chaotic state of mind when she brought her the tidings, which called for discussions - *Nefer knew this* - and today would be no different. *If she was persuasive enough though, and her Mama sent her to the Council, then a little decorum might well be worth it.*

At the thought of her Mama's frown, she pushed at the flaring width of her jade-encrusted necklace to settle it back into its proper resting place across her collarbones and tentatively rubbed her nape instead of her head. Her mother was most insistent that people of all the four quadrants would know exactly whom they were gazing at wherever and whenever - and here entered decorum again. *Why First Companion Nafretiri worried so much that the Sabén-Heshep would ever forget the face of the Watchéran's Best-loved Wife or Daughter, Nefer did not understand, because people did not forget. Ever. But her mother had come from afar. She still jealously continued to guard her position, and would in all likelihood probably never forget that she'd been intended a mere tribute…*

Nefer snatched another fat beetle from the wall and looped it at Seih-rahrat as she resumed her purpose, passing under the lintel and feeling a shift in the pressure of air and temperature the moment she passed from the maze-warded corridor onto the roofless inner court. The sharpness of light was instant, the contrast blinding, but with a contented growl from the old lizard riding in her shadow, she embraced the feeling, forcing the squint from her eyes.

The Golden Eye was still on ascend, bright like burnished copper afire in a pure azure sky to reflect off the smooth square-cut marble beneath her feet, but a blast of warm air rolled over her, soothing the lingering tendrils of coldness inside and she sighed, close to happiness with the heartbeat of life that once more surrounded her.

She'd have to cross the plaza to get to the Royal Complex but she didn't mind. Around her, the inner court sprawled like a giant maze, the elegant creamy-pink stone flawed-by-silver something uniquely native to these lands, whilst the smoky marbles used for the abundant relief-carvings had had to be quarried beyond the Sabén-Heshep by the ancient Fhearan Masters back when they'd still walked on land and embraced air. She thought it a shame they could no longer visit for she should have dearly loved to see the supposed splendour of their halls as described in the annals, but the Veils had been raised a long, long time ago - and all former alliances voided.

Nefer voided her own fickle dreams too. If she wanted to get to her mother's wing of the Royal Complex, the most direct route ran straight across the giant courtyard and for the purpose of appearances, she floated her steps, adjusting to seem unhurried.

There were people aplenty about their day out here and they did not neglect her, though she in turn ignored them and theirs, as she was met with a seemingly unending number of inclined chins, respectfully bent backs and a general miscellaneous assortment of small honours. It remained little more than a nuisance to be expected. *It was decorum. And this time she had to make them believe…*

Past the boulder-sized hanging baskets of cascading flowers and palm-filled planters - some of which complimented statues fifteen hand span or more, some of which formed arrangements of their own from pots as tall as the humps of an adult Grey Ri-u'dat – Nefer'Kemnebit maintain an outward indifference to the mass of lush vegetation and opulent of wealth.

The enticing colours of the meticulously sunken fish ponds, rimmed in gold and jade - brimming with blessed lotus blossoms and silver-sided Koi - usually tugged at her gaze a good handful of times before she found herself past their tranquil presence, but today she did not permit herself to stop and let her mind wander with the lazy sway of the giant fish as they rested near-motionless amongst the undulating pond blossoms. *The Council must understand. This time the title of Living Daughter of the best-loved Suten Himé, Nafretiri the Pale, had to count for something. He-Who-Is* treasured his golden-hued foreign beauty and the name of Royal Wife was bestowed on Nafretiri alone. At seventy-one, Nefer had never sought to push her pedigree to further any sort of understanding with the Council but maybe she was finally ready? *If only she'd dare.*

The idea of something red tugged at the periphery of her attention. *Red as deep as royal blood…*

She looked to the left; sharply – her mind focusing on the crimson awning stretched wide across the far end of the plaza, affording shade. *Red…? Royal red? Here?*

Nefer'Kemnebit felt her heart plummet, but the sight that greeted her allowed her little room to deny what she already knew. It brought her to a shuddering halt mid-glide.

He was there and she saw him: the Sabén-Heshep ruler and protector, the Watchéran; the Ancient One: He-Who-Is the eternal God descended, her Sire. Her Father.

Imprisoned

Solancei gritted her teeth, a small activity that vaguely inspired the vain hope she hadn't lost any after all - because there did not appear to be any gaps. It was a ridiculous, tiny victory, hardly of pressing worth, and yet…

Call her conceited, but she'd prefer her smile the way it was. With all teeth present and unbroken.

She killed the small burst of erratic elation, her spirit not quite in it, despite swagger or pretence. *Simaro… what was his game? He'd broken the one sacred rule in the game of no rules? Why?*

A strange notion of embarrassment swept through her, loaded with a corrosive portion of venomous resentment – though whether the latter was as much for herself as it was for her cheating bastard opponent, she couldn't quite have said.

She cringed for the flaws within. *Yes, Klaas had trained her, but…*

Simaro had thrown six fully-armed men into her path after she'd already been tired and unbalanced from the crazed development at the Jackal. *How to deal with that?*

Mentally she shook her head at the perplexity but there would be no hiding behind excuses. *She should have done better.* Klaas would insist that she should have made good her escape regardless! A Shield was more than a simple soldier; being a Shield meant thinking on your feet, turning every disadvantage to serve your own purpose, twisting the flow of events and violence to keeping your footing on a slippery surface where others might fall down or worse. *And who'd have thought…? A few inches of muddy sludge and here she was.* Simple treachery of the weather notwithstanding, Simaro had shifted the understanding of her own limits, not to mention staked several question marks through her purpose and the safety of anyone within his immediate reach, including Iambre. She did not like it. In fact, it made her sick just thinking...

She closed her eyes tightly against the events that replayed across her peace of mind, but she could not cut them out; couldn't cut out Simaro standing over her. *Maybe if he hadn't crashed his haitu into her as though to fell a stubborn oak tree. Maybe...*

But of course he'd wanted to prove a point; that seemed of importance to him - she understood that very clearly now. He'd caught up to his men, courtesy of that damn whistle, and he'd wanted her to know that he'd taken the win after all! Had wanted her to be aware...

Solancei forced her mind blank and clenched her teeth again, but the headache thumped merrily, and shavings of anger began to smoulder in her core. She would never again make the mistake assuming that Simaro might have an ounce of chivalry in him! Never! Of all the people she'd squared up with, he was the least honourable. *Which seemed ironic...*

A small sound of luckless mirth escaped her. *He'd set his men on her, chased her down like some filthy thief and never blinked as they injured her. Arbar'Chi slay them with pest – who did that?* She couldn't seem to prevent her own disbelief; couldn't help the chilling notion of consequence. *And as for that trowel's son with the whistle!*

Solancei seemed to recall little after that, so she must have been out when they'd dragged her here. *But for how long? And just 'where' was 'where'?* With things developing so rapidly, and the way they had, she must question if Klaas even knew the truth of what had happened?

She swallowed painfully, shavings of anxiety offering no answers. *She could well be on her own in this. She hoped not, but-*

Solancei winced softly and swallowed a sliver of pain as her ribs moved. This was a disaster. The fact that Klaas Mehadja had failed to warn her of something as important as the unpredictable psyche of a jackal fight opponent seemed like a rather large oversight on her mentor's behalf, and it just didn't sit well. Klaas was the master of her trade and somehow Solancei did not think her mentor capable of any oversight – no matter how insignificant. *Which left her where?*

Head pounding, she found it hard to string theory together. She supposed her mentor's ignorance was plausible; Simaro's personal involvement in the fight hadn't been confirmed until she'd laid eyes on him in that backyard, so maybe Klaas hadn't thought…

She licked split lips and winced again. *Hadn't thought what? Gods be damned but what could Simaro possibly want from her? Yes, he was angry that she'd bested him and cut his little set-up to shreds – that much she'd be a fool not to see - but to keep her imprisoned? Locked away like this?*

Solancei's head ached but twisting thoughts and recriminating questions wouldn't let her rest. The sobering theory that Simaro might know of her true identity kept rising up like a rearing cobra ready to strike her dead with fear for the implications, but she kept the poisonous possibility at bay because this remained the most impossible of scenarios. *She was Cheska del'Duvraska from New Wood. It was a sound alias. It was unbroken; substantiated.*

Or at least, that was what the Chief had sworn to her repeatedly, and in this she trusted. He would not be able to hold her as 'leverage', nor for 'bribery'. Her existence would be denied by the Court, for indeed most of the Court knew nothing of this extracurricular business, and even fewer knew about her title of Shield. Allegations made – whether true or false –

would most assuredly be refuted with the righteous outrage of men who knew no better. No, there had to be-

'Clunk!'

The muffled sound broke into Solancei's reverie so unexpectedly that she thought it another figment of her imagination. The leaping of her stomach told her differently though, and her heart seemed to miss a beat as silence as black as the surrounding air seemed to creep all over her like the groping tentacles of a hunting fantasy monster that slowly burned the life from its quarry with every jabbing touch.

Forgetting how much it'd hurt only moments ago, habit made her chew on her lip and she hissed. The small pain was not important though and cocking her head just a fraction to one side, she concentrated till she thought herself gone daft because, for long aching moments, all she heard was her own straining heartbeat as she laboured to keep quiet. Then came the unmistakable sound of keys playing a staccato tune against their neighbours as someone walked at a steady pace, and though the sounds were barely there, she was no longer in doubt. *Somebody was coming.* The metallic tingle was growing leisurely louder; clearer, framed by another sound now, perhaps the whisper of footfalls?

It made her nerves stand on edge – like quills vibrating against the inside of her skin, threatening to pierce her sanity if she did not hold firm and there was a coldness within her… *growing*…

She couldn't feel the Veranto though; she felt as indefinitely blind to the skill as ever; there was nothing there to connect with; nothing to delve into. It was detrimental. She needed to forge a link, but her ability did not comply. She licked her lips again, glad of the pain now. It made her sharp: in lieu of what the State of Veranto could've provided, at least it proved more than enough to solidify the idea of 'company' into reality, yet-

Yet it was almost too much. Feeling like a cornered animal, her stomach twisted as abrupt, new fear seemed to rise in colour within. It was crystal. Blues with the fractions of icy white and silver recalled from the winters of her childhood, but in the coldness, there was a sense of wrath rising too - and for a blink, she knew not which to fear the most: that, what was moving towards her without? Or the razor-edge of that, which was rising within? She could barely move; she had no way of defending herself; and-

A strand of fire shot through her with a silent twang that might have sounded like a bow string releasing had it been audible. It was a slow, liquid feeling; it was the brutal gut-flinching, muscle-wrenching release experienced when a dislocated joint was reset; it was a mental re-ordering like a field surgeon's scalpel slicing up stitches gone too tight on a wound not yet healed... *all just so right*... and yet...

And yet also so terribly wrong because there was 'conflict' now: a roaring fire pitched against endless frost.

She felt her eyes roll back in her head as the eruption between the two diametrical opposites flared, holding her on the cusp of an imaginary precipice, every sinew in her tightening till she somehow lingered on the knife-edge of unconsciousness. As a sense of salvation beckoned, a perception of abandon rode her - but she wanted to fall into death rather than embrace that which she felt there in her core beyond the normal reach of sanity, incandescent but alien.

Something ripped – killing pain and fear. In the presence of a blink, her core seemed an ancient wound; there was a slash like a beast savaging its kill: a final snarl that sounded like it came from her own mind as well as from her lips, then...

Reaction was all and as her spirit reached, her mind centred, and-

Bliss engulfed her. In less than a beat of the heart, she felt as light as air, as collected as a veteran senator, as deadly as a blade in the hand of a white assassin... *this... oh mercy... this she knew!*

Issuing a hiss of disbelieving pleasure, she almost cringed in anticipation of the pain to come but it was void. *Mercy, it was void! Mercy...*

Elation of a differing kind rolled through her. *Somehow...? Somehow she'd just grappled for the State of Veranto as though it was her right, and just like that – after all the failures and the mediocre sense of ability – she'd succeeded!*

Euphoria made it impossible for her to stay still but there was no backlash, only the familiar feelings of clarity and calm that she'd come to expect.

That was almost too much too. After the strange attack of – *well of whatever the fleck that had been? She did not know how to class the success; didn't know what the fleck that feeling of discord had meant for her* - but it had broken something, or maybe mended it, and well...

Gods, but she'd thought herself wrong somehow but it was not so! Mercifully not so! She'd just been too tired; too distressed - possibly with other matters - to find the needed peace within, but here... now... pushed and without choice?

As if she'd just drunk an entire cup of Klaas' brew for head-sore, her mind seemed to cast away the shadows of fatigue and confusion. It brought a feeling akin to healing into her and though she knew it was nothing but illusion, she sighed with weary relief. Now was also a time for caution, of course: she mustn't abuse her new 'cloak of lies' – not even if she felt good as new. *The injuries were still there, masked, and would be demanding a price of her later. But that was for later. After you get the fleck out of this place!*

A jangle of keys and a few unmistakable sounds of scuffed footsteps drew her back to reality. No time seemed to have passed. Somehow amidst the debilitating attack and her effortless success to reach into the State of Veranto, she'd felt hours fly by in the wink of an eye, but nothing had changed. Company was still due, that couldn't be ignored.

She pulled at her bonds but they were solid. *Now what?*

Suddenly unsure, a sliver of nerves sliced open imaginary wounds, sending a quiver through the Veranto and she yanked herself a tighter focus, alarmed that the precarious link could still be lost in a heartbeat, just as had happened as of late with disturbing frequency.

Yet, she did not wish to greet whoever this was on her knees. She might be injured but she did not want to appear weak, and though she hoped this had just been some fey kind of misunderstanding, nevertheless...

Shaking with the strain, ignoring the toil of warning-bells, she forced effort into legs and arms, pushing her limbs to co-operate and raise her up off the ground. It took her to the knees, then she paused in caution. She'd laid across a groove in the rock wherein a shallow puddle had home: a fact gone unnoticed until this very moment where the still-fresh, wet streak across her leather released smells of stale mineral-rich water to battle the fading stench of ammonia.

It introduced new strange notions in her mind - for a moment she seemed to be outside herself again, *like she was dreaming*, but this she recognised. The sensation of masked injuries was ever-peculiar: not a good reminder of the truth, really; and knowing that she would've never been able to do such this impossible thing without the aid of the Veranto, she whispered a word of prayer and thanks to the Goddess of Luck. *If she dropped the link now – either through slip-up or lapse of strength – it would be disastrous. This was all she had. Gods, but she hoped it was enough. She hoped and prayed.*

She relinquished the need to shiver, but it was as though she'd never known a problem in her life. The ability stayed fresh, never wavering, never glitching - her spirit was centred, her mind focused; the link was a spidery support, fine yet solidly anchored, and for a moment she allowed herself to relax, but not for long. She would have to gather her faculties and prepare for the-Gods-only-knew-what-confrontation. *She needed to push this.*

Pulling her focus deep, turning her mind inwards, she exhaled and laboured to stand. It appeared that the floor was relatively level, but taking no chances in the pitch dark she moved with a slow deliberateness that felt less bold than her situation warranted - still, the vacuum of her current world seemed to suit the caution and she gained a measure of hope. *The Veranto didn't even waver either. Merciful Gods... she might just be okay. If she could only retain the link...*

Stumbling slightly as she took a few halting steps forward, she nursed her injured ribs, inching towards a feeling of control when her hesitant shuffle brought her in touch with vertical rock. To her splayed fingers it portrayed the same rough, uneven finish as the floor beneath her boots and yet relief flooded. *She was standing – slightly dizzy sure, and favouring her injury, yes - but the State of Veranto was hers again! It was hers!*

Head resting against the cool wall as the spinning seemed to momentarily intensify, she listened for a good few beats to the heavy footsteps marching towards her. She heard them clearly now, uniform and even; without urgency, yet with a hint of purpose. *Soldiers perhaps?*

It was a valid theory but though she held the Veranto, she could not focus on the idea. She needed to get out of here. But how? There was no

184

time. Nowhere to hide. The salty tune of bouncing keys seemed to add a strange rhythm to the fall of footsteps; for the first time, Solancei saw the vaguest glimmer of orange light filter through a section of wall directly opposite. *Light...*

She issued a harsh breath, emotions flying higher than commonly experienced when the Veranto hugged her. The illumination was barely there but in the complete darkness, the small comfort brought a sharp memory of everything that mattered: Iambre, Klaas, South-Point, Tuxama, her escaping this hole, this predicament...

Distractions... all distractions! Again unusual when delving into a link, she clawed back strength, smoothing out the kinks. *It wasn't foolproof. Nothing seemed to be these days.* With every new sound, the sense of being cornered flared like a second heartbeat and she found herself taking an unwitting step backwards as the feeling began tightening her chest, somehow battling the shield of Veranto as though it might weaken the link enough to cause catastrophic failure.

She clenched her teeth hard against the sensation.

Another step of retreat left her mouth suddenly dry with the strain of hanging on and out of nowhere it brought back memories of times long past, when she - still only an Adept - had been trying so very hard to find the perfect balance between the extreme possibilities of Veranto. She hadn't faced such uncertainty in a very long time; she was long past those wobbly attempts of her early years - yet the possibilities of a 'disaster' still haunted, because lately-

She ripped her thoughts in half to force a smile in the darkness. *You have the right to name yourself 'Master',* she scolded herself, *now let that count for something and the rest be hanged! Gods, might not even Iambre's*

T'lexara Corunan Vitalioni be permitted a few jittery heartbeats once in a while? In spite popular opinion, are you not as Human as any?

She drew a steadying breath, releasing the wall to stand unaided. *No weakness. She'd show no weakness.*

Folding her hands in a casual display of ease to spite the rope, she applied all her will to the purpose of dispersing that lingering sense of clammy unease. It partly worked. *Well, no one was infallible; the stomping boots were closing fast...*

For a moment her heartbeat seemed to match the cadence, but as torchlight flared outside her cell to outline the contours of a door she hadn't been previously aware of, the feet came to an abrupt halt and every ounce of her seemed to grow still like a gathering force before the release of the command to sally forth. It was a form of control, but not.

A worm of her earlier anger helping her now, she reached for the feeling, deepening her resentment.

As expected, it served her well. She guessed it always did. Whoever had come for her, had the keys and she wanted out of here! And if they had weapons...

Backing up slowly, she reacted from pure instinct when she heard the strained breathing of several men accompany the sharp jingle of keys as one was selected, then inserted and twisted to unlock the door with a dour scrape. Bizarrely; vainly; she suddenly wished she didn't stink like an old latrine, but it seemed a by-product of a thought that should've belonged to someone else; someone not here in this cell.

Calm settled around her then, like a mantle of fine gossamer, steadying her nerves and centering her attention. As she might have expected, the brief pause before the door swung inwards seemed unbearably long, but then a glare of light cut her vision to shreds, all but obliterating the darkness.

Blinking furiously to adjust, Solancei shielded watering eyes. She was acutely aware of people entering the cell, but the glare had her at a disadvantage and she was not quite able to determine numbers in the blurry maze of light and dark, hobnailed boots and swirling cloaks. She figured her initial guess seemed probable, though. Her visitors must be soldiers. She could glean as much from the small actions she was able to decipher before her eyes teared up again, yet looking through the lace pattern of her interlocking fingers she tried again and was eventually able to identify two shoulder-to-shoulder torch bearers who appeared to move in unison to place their fluttering lights high into a couple of rust-covered wall brackets before flanking the door like a pair of silent honour guards.

Again, she blinked rapidly, but her eyes were adjusting now, lending her a rough idea of the confines of her cell as well, and…

Rats, but even for a prison, this was poor. It was of a rock so dark that even the presence of light seemed unable to battle away the deep shadows - yet not so the glistening trails of moisture that decorated the oppressive stone-like runnels of tears on an ancient face, all of which stood out like silvered slime under the flickering torches. Her eyes rolled across the fissures cutting the floor as though Arbar'Chi himself had slashed at the core with his poisonous talons gouging out scars in the bedrock; the space horrifically generous, nevertheless, she did not want to stay here. She did not want-

She steered her eyes back to the additional men filing round and filling the space with bodies and breaths. In the golden torch glare, she couldn't glean much. They were all shrouded against the chill and facing forward, two almost on either side of her, whilst the other two – more torch bearers, she realised – had melted back with the shadows they'd only half-successfully dispersed, to stand shoulder-to-shoulder with the men at the door. Then a movement directly outside the cell caught her eye and Solancei squinted, looking past the soldiers to find a lone figure paused to inspect.

It made her want to twitch. She recognised the stance in a blink, even if the broad tallness had been smothered by a thick cloak that revealed little of the person underneath.

Seemed her flecking-cheat jackal fight opponent had come to heap insult to pain in the flesh! Oh – bloody – yay!

***

Thank you for reading☺

The story will continue in Episode 3: A Perspective of Death

Available now

****

Post Script from the author

Hi there!

If you enjoyed this book (or any of the others ☺) I'd really love it if you would take just two minutes to leave a review on your media of choice(s). It's matters because not only do I get feedback on my product, which is invaluable for me to learn and grow as an author, but it may also help other readers understand if this book is for them and – very importantly – that it's okay to take a chance on an indie publication.

*****

And finally…

Curious about the world of Ostravah?

Want to keep in touch?

For glossaries, maps, and more, please visit my official author website

Here you can also join my **exclusive newsletter** 'Thrills & Spills' to receive extra insider info, updates, freebies, exclusive offers and giveaways,

www.llthomsen.com

Also feel free to contact me via…

I would always love to hear from you and all constructive feedback is welcome!

facebook.com/themissingshield/

facebook.com/linda.thomsen.12979

twitter.com/LLThomsen1

instagram.com/llthomsen/?hl=en

pinterest.co.uk/llthomsen7589/

goodreads.com/LLThomsen

***

The Missing Shield Series

This story begins in Episode 1 of The Missing Shield.

Below is the full list of books in the series in order of release.

- ➢ A Change of Rules – Episode 1
- ➢ Unexpected Bargain – Episode 2
- ➢ A Perspective of Death – Episode 3
- ➢ Running the Gauntlet – Episode 4
- ➢ Notions of Risk – Episode 5
- ➢ The Final Card - Episode 6
- ➢ The Lure of an Ancient Fable – Episode 7
- ➢ All in a Day's Work – Episode 8

And coming up soon in 2020...

- ➢ The Way Star –Episode 9
- ➢ All Thieves' Honour – Episode 10
- ➢ The Neidar Ba'raie – Episode 11

This will complete The Missing Shield – Vol 1 of 'The Veil Keepers Quest'.

***

New!

Also NOW available: **The Missing Shield, Part 1** - Author's Preferred Edition box set, which includes episodes 1 – 6.
Only available as eBook and on KU.

***

*****

www.ingramcontent.com/pod-product-compliance
Lightning Source LLC
Chambersburg PA
CBHW051509170626
46811CB00002B/726